A Bond
with Death

Also by Bill Crider
in Large Print:

Red, White and Blue Murder
Galveston Gunman
Medicine Show
Ryan Rides Back
A Time for Hanging

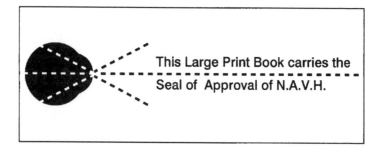

A Bond with Death

Bill Crider

WHEELER PUBLISHING

Published in 2005 by arrangement with St. Martin's Press, LLC.

Wheeler Large Print Compass.

The text of this Large Print edition is unabridged.
Other aspects of the book may vary from the original edition.

Set in 16 pt. Plantin by Christina S. Huff.

Printed in the United States on permanent paper.

Library of Congress Cataloging-in-Publication Data

Crider, Bill, 1941–
    A bond with death / Bill Crider.
      p. cm.
    ISBN 1-58724-868-9 (lg. print : hc : alk. paper)
    1. Good, Sally (Fictitious character) — Fiction.
2. English teachers — Fiction. 3. College teachers —
Fiction. 4. Women teachers — Fiction. 5. Texas —
Fiction. 6. Large type books. I. Title.
PS3553.R497B65 2005
  813′.54—dc22   2004043129

For Terry Thompson
(aka Mama ClueFest)

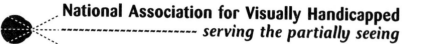

National Association for Visually Handicapped
---------------------- serving the partially seeing

As the Founder/CEO of NAVH, the only national health agency solely devoted to those who, although not totally blind, have an eye disease which could lead to serious visual impairment, I am pleased to recognize Thorndike Press* as one of the leading publishers in the large print field.

Founded in 1954 in San Francisco to prepare large print textbooks for partially seeing children, NAVH became the pioneer and standard setting agency in the preparation of large type.

Today, those publishers who meet our standards carry the prestigious "Seal of Approval" indicating high quality large print. We are delighted that Thorndike Press is one of the publishers whose titles meet these standards. We are also pleased to recognize the significant contribution Thorndike Press is making in this important and growing field.

Lorraine H. Marchi, L.H.D.
Founder/CEO
NAVH

* Thorndike Press encompasses the following imprints: Thorndike, Wheeler, Walker and Large Print Press.

1

Sally Good blamed the Internet for a lot of things.

She blamed it for the e-mail messages that flooded her mailbox at the Hughes Community College address. Most of the messages were worthless spam, and they made outrageous promises to increase her bust size by two or three cups, make her irresistible through the power of pheromones, allow her to lose twenty to thirty pounds in ten days, find her the perfect soulmate, make her rich by helping her set up a "simple home business," or provide her with a platinum credit card with $5,000 in unsecured credit. Among other things.

She blamed it for putting canned research papers on the screens of students who went looking for a plot summary and found a complete research paper that they could buy, teaching them that it was easier to pay to have someone do their work for them than to do it themselves.

But most of all she blamed it for having made it easy for someone to find out that she was related, by marriage, to a witch. And for making it so easy to send a distorted version of that information to practically everyone at the college and the entire community it served.

"It doesn't reflect well on the college at all," President Fieldstone said, "having one's ancestor hanged for witchcraft."

"Sarah Good wasn't my ancestor," Sally said. "She was my husband's ancestor, and my husband's been dead for eight years now. Besides, you surely don't believe she was actually a witch."

Fieldstone didn't say anything, so Sally continued.

"Even if she was, all that hysteria happened over three hundred years ago."

On July 19, 1692, to be exact, the same day that Elizabeth Howe, Sarah Wildes, Rebecca Nurse, and Susannah Martin had been hanged along with Sarah Good. Sally had seen Sarah's gravestone once upon a time, while on vacation with her late husband. And of course she'd read about how Sarah Good had gone defiantly to the gallows, never having admitted that she was a witch, and how she had called out to one of her accusers, "You are a liar. I am no more a witch than you are a wizard, and if you take away my life God will give you blood to drink," a curse that Nathaniel Hawthorne had appropriated without credit for use in *The House of the Seven Gables*, which Sally had read when she was a junior in high school.

The fact that Sarah Good's curse came true, Noyes later having died with internal hemorrhaging, bleeding profusely at the mouth like Judge Pyncheon in Hawthorne's novel, probably did a lot to convince people at the time that Sarah had been very much the witch she had denied being.

But while Sally was certain that none of that had much to do with her and the present, Fieldstone didn't seem convinced as he sat there behind his big, smooth, tidy desk, the top of which would have reflected his own image back at him had he glanced down at it. It was so clean and smooth, in fact, that Sally wondered if dust could even stick to it. The extreme cleanliness made Sally cringe when she thought of her own, which was covered with student papers, some of them, maybe most of them, ungraded; books, memos, letters, and maybe a Hershey wrapper or two. Just the kind of desk a witch would probably have.

Sally sat across from Fieldstone in an

uncomfortable but expensive leather chair, wishing that she were somewhere else, maybe in a committee meeting of some kind. And she hated committee meetings.

"It doesn't matter how long ago it was," Fieldstone said, "or whether I believe in witchcraft. It doesn't even really matter who Sarah Good was related to."

Whom, Sally thought. Not *who.* But that was what came of ending a sentence with a preposition.

"What matters," Fieldstone continued, "is what people think. We live in a very conservative part of the state, and people here are touchy about things like that. There have been several attempts to get those Harry Potter books removed from the public library, as I'm sure you know."

Sally knew. She was one of the people who'd spoken out against the removal of the books.

"And," Fieldstone went on, "you undoubtedly remember the episode with the satanic painting right here at the college."

Sally remembered that little episode, and her involvement in it, all too well.

"It wasn't a satanic painting," she said. "It was just a picture of a goat. That's all it was."

"Possibly. But it caused quite an uproar.

We can't have that kind of thing, especially now that we're trying to pass a bond."

Hughes Community College had a fairly prosperous district, but the district was small, and Hughes was hemmed in on all sides by other community colleges, all of which were in direct competition for students. Fieldstone believed that to attract more students, the college needed to update the buildings and equipment, build new classroom space, and improve the athletic facilities. That would take money, money the college didn't have. Hence the bond proposal.

"There are some people in the community who are already organizing against the college," Fieldstone said. "This witch business won't help."

The people of whom he spoke, Sally knew, included some former members of the college faculty who, for whatever reason, had decided to take a stand against the place where they'd made a reasonably good living for quite a number of years before they had elected to retire. Or, in some cases, before they had been more or less forced to retire. Some of them held grudges, especially those in the latter category. One of them even held a grudge against Sally.

"What am I supposed to do?" Sally asked. "Apologize for my husband's ancestor?"

"That might be a good first step. And while you're at it, you can repudiate witchcraft."

Sally thought he might be joking, but then she noticed the tight set of his mouth and the white knuckles of the hands clasped in front of him on the slick, dustless desktop.

"I can't believe we're having this conversation," she said.

Fieldstone's mouth tightened even further, until it was just a razor-thin line in his face.

"The college needs the bond issue to pass," he said. Even when he spoke, his lips were so thin that they could hardly be seen. "Everyone on the faculty has to work together to be sure that it does."

It sounded a lot like a threat to Sally, who didn't respond well to threats. She said, "I'll do all I can to help pass the bond. I'll make calls, I'll write letters, I'll talk to the civic clubs. But I won't apologize for something that happened more than three hundred years ago. I won't 'repudiate witchcraft,' and I won't criticize Sarah Good, who was railroaded in the first place, like a lot of other women in 1692."

Fieldstone was a graduate of Texas A&M University. The school colors were maroon and white, and at that moment Fieldstone's face above his starched white shirt made him look very school-spirited indeed, Sally thought.

"I'm sure you'll do everything you can," Fieldstone said, his voice a little hoarse. "That will be all, for the moment."

Sally stood up, thought about saying one more thing, didn't, and got out of there.

She arrived at her American literature class a couple of minutes late, having had to go back to her office for her textbook and grade book. She found the text on the desk under a set of pop tests (graded, thank goodness), and the grade book was in the top drawer, the one that could be locked, probably *should* be locked, but never was. Sally worried that someday, someone might steal the grade book, but she couldn't bring herself to lock the drawer. Besides, she'd lost the key years ago.

Conversation was buzzing when she arrived at the classroom, but it stopped the instant she entered. It wasn't that the students were eager to discuss the assignment, which was Poe's "The Philosophy of Composition" and "The Raven." They wanted to talk about something entirely different.

It was Wayne Compton who got the ball rolling, as usual. He was a short, stocky young man with red hair cut short and a red face to match. He sat in the front row and seldom read the assignment. Even when he did, he never remembered much about it. Nevertheless, he loved class discussion. It didn't seem to make much difference to him whether he was on the right track or not, just as long as he got to talk.

"Dr. Good," he said, as soon as Sally had finished marking the roll in her grade book, "is it true?"

"Is what true?" Sally asked, though she had a terrible feeling that she knew exactly what he was asking.

Wayne looked around the room. The other students had expectant looks on their faces, and Sally presumed the looks weren't the result of enthusiasm for what she might have to say about Poe's essay and poem.

"Well," Wayne said, "you remember that stuff we read at the beginning of the semester?"

"What 'stuff' would that be, Wayne? Anne Bradstreet's poems? Winthrop's history?"

14

"No, that other stuff. About the witches."

"The excerpts from Cotton Mather's *Wonders of the Invisible World*."

"Yeah, that stuff. About the witches. You remember that."

Probably a lot better than you do, Sally thought. She said, "I remember, Wayne."

"Well, you didn't mention that you were related to them."

"Related to whom?"

"To the witches," Wayne said. "A bunch of us got an e-mail about it."

Wayne looked around again, and several of the other students nodded.

"So is it true?" Wayne wanted to know, turning back to her.

Sally explained that it wasn't true and that while her late husband had been distantly related to a woman named Sarah Good, who had indeed been executed for witchcraft, Sally herself wasn't related to her in any way except by marriage, which didn't count.

"So what did they do to her?" Wayne asked. "To Sarah Good, I mean."

"I'm sure you remember, Wayne. What was the preferred method for executing witches in the American colonies?"

"Hanging," Wayne said. "You told us they never burned anybody or anything."

"They hanged Sarah Good, too, Wayne, like they did the others."

"Except for that guy you told us about, the one they pressed to death."

"Yes," Sally said, surprised that Wayne remembered so much. "Giles Corey. Except for him, the witches were hanged."

"And you're saying that Sarah Good was innocent?"

"They were all innocent," Sally said. "Eventually they were all pardoned by the state, the last of them in 2001."

"They were pardoned after they'd been dead more than three hundred years?"

"Some of them."

"Didn't help 'em much, did it," Wayne said.

"Not at all. But my husband appreciated it, and I'm sure the other descendants did, too."

"But the e-mail was a hoax?" Wayne said.

"That's right," Sally told him. "Imagine that. An e-mail hoax. What will they think of next?"

A couple of the students grinned.

"Now," Sally said, "I think it's time we discussed today's assignment. But before we begin, does anyone have any questions?"

A hand shot into the air. Sally sighed.

"Yes, Wayne?" she said.

16

The day's discussion had gone better than Sally thought it would. Wayne had read at least part of the assignment, or maybe he just remembered "The Raven" from high school. Some of the other students had things to say about the points in "The Philosophy of Composition" as they related to the Poe stories the class had discussed earlier in the week.

So Sally was in a good mood when she went back to her office. She seldom closed her office door during the day, and Jack Neville was sitting by her desk in the uncomfortable chair that she had put there for visitors.

"Have you heard?" Jack asked before she could even get in the door.

Sally walked on into her office and put the books on top of the papers on her desk.

"Heard what?" she asked.

"The Garden Gnome died last night," Jack said.

2

The Garden Gnome was a person, not a statue. He was, or had been, Harold Curtin, whose unfortunate resemblance to a gnome had given him his nickname. He didn't wear a tall red peaked cap or red pointed shoes, but then he'd been dubbed the Garden Gnome for his physical appearance, not for his attire.

He was short and stout, and he had a white beard. His face was often an alarming shade of red, as if he might suffer from high blood pressure, though that hadn't been the cause, as Sally had discovered.

Curtin had been a teacher in the English department at HCC when Sally arrived to take over as department chair. She had been appalled when she glanced over his student evaluations at the end of her first semester. They weren't just the worst evaluations in the department; they were the worst in the college. They were, in fact, the worst Sally had ever seen.

Students generally looked upon the day

when an evaluation was done as an opportunity to get out of class early, so they did the multiple choice part of the questionnaire as quickly as possible and skipped the optional section that invited written comments.

But not in Curtin's case. His students disliked him so much that they would rather take the time to write a few comments than have an extra ten minutes between classes. And the comments weren't kind:

He treats us like ants in his domain.

He's never prepared for class. Most of the time he doesn't even know what the assignment was supposed to be.

His tests don't make any sense, and he never grades them. I think he just makes up his grades and puts them in his book.

We had to write five essays, but he only gave back one of them. There was no grade on it and he didn't mark any errors.

He tells us we're idiots all the time.

After reading those and a few dozen similar remarks, Sally went to Dean Naylor's office. Naylor was a large, cheerful man and one of his besetting sins was his outgoing nature. Sally didn't feel that there was anything wrong with liking people, but Naylor was a hugger. There was nothing

19

sexist about his hugging. He hugged men and women indiscriminately, but Sally preferred to maintain a little more decorum. She usually maneuvered around the office and kept a chair between herself and Naylor whenever possible. Recently, in the face of some criticism from higher up, he had managed to curtail his hugging, but in the days when Curtin had been in the college's employ, Naylor had been for the most part unrestrained.

On the day of her visit about Curtin, Sally sat down in the visitor's chair before Naylor could get around the desk to hug her and said, "What's going on with Harold Curtin?"

"Harold Curtin? Nothing's going on with Harold. He's been here for years."

"I know. But I'm not talking about how long he's been here. I'm talking about his evaluations."

"His evaluations? Do you mean his student evaluations? What about them?"

Naylor was perhaps a perfect dean. He could dance around a topic for hours without ever getting to the heart of it, and he could avoid giving a straight answer better than anyone Sally had ever dealt with. He was wasted at the community college, she often thought. He should have been in the state legislature. Congress, even. Or maybe working as the president's press secretary.

"His student evaluations are terrible," Sally said. "He's ranked lower than anyone else here, and the students' written comments about him are scathing."

Naylor clasped his hands over his stomach and leaned back in his chair.

"Well," he said, "as you're certainly aware, students often don't know how to do an evaluation properly. Instructors spend years in college learning their discipline, and then they hone the craft for more years in the classroom. When they present a lesson, they're doing something that they've trained for and practiced for a long, long time. On the other hand, students don't take evaluations very seriously. They rush through them, and they hardly ever even think about the questions they're answering and how those answers might affect an instructor's career."

He paused for a breath, and Sally managed to get a word in before he started again. She knew he could go on like that all day if she let him get away with it.

"The students took this evaluation seriously," she said. "I think we can be certain of that. I'd like to see Mr. Curtin's evaluations from previous years, and I'd like for you to have a look at some of these comments."

She handed the green sheets of paper across the desk to Naylor. He took them and shuffled them around, but he put them down with only a casual glance.

"As you know if you've read your policy manual," he said, "all evaluations come to this office for filing after the department chairs have looked them over. A printed copy of the evaluation results for each department is sent to the department chair, who then forwards copies to individual instructors."

"I know the process, but I wasn't here last year when evaluations were done."

"Your predecessor, Dr. Barton, followed the procedure, I'm sure."

Sally didn't see what the process had to do with what she was talking about. She was about to say so, but Naylor didn't give her a chance to break in.

"I'm sure Mr. Curtin has seen his evaluations and knows how they stack up against others in his department. He's probably working hard to correct any deficiencies in his performance, and we'll no doubt see some improvement soon."

"He's had a whole semester to improve," Sally said. "If his evaluations were any worse last year, he should have been fired. And these are so bad that they couldn't have been worse last year. I'd like to see them."

"As you may know, they're stored in the vault."

What Sally knew was that there wasn't really a vault, though the storeroom was often called by that name for some reason.

"So I've heard. They should be easy enough to find."

"I could have one of the secretaries look for them, but I'm afraid they won't be easy to locate. The evaluations are stored in cardboard boxes, but there's really no filing system. I'm afraid they're simply put into the boxes when they arrive in my office and then transferred to the vault after instructors have had a chance to look over them."

"I'd still like to see them."

Naylor looked at her as if wondering why she'd ever been hired in the first place.

"Very well. I'll have Wynona look for them as soon as she has a chance."

Wynona Reed was in the outer office, and if Sally was any judge of character, she'd heard every word of the conversation between Sally and Naylor. Sally hadn't bothered to close the door, but she didn't think it would have made any difference had she done so. She knew Wynona would never stoop to something so obvious as putting a stethoscope to the door, but the secretary always seemed to know what was being said in Naylor's office, closed door or not. Maybe she listened on the intercom. Except that there wasn't one. Mental telepathy? Sally couldn't figure it out.

"When do you think she'll have a chance to look for them?" Sally asked.

"You can ask her when you leave," Naylor said, which was as close to a curt dismissal as Sally had ever received from him. She got up and thanked him for his time before going to the other office, where Wynona sat staring at a computer screen.

"It's not that hard to find the evaluations," Wynona said before Sally had a chance to ask. "I'll get them for you this afternoon. He just doesn't want you to see them because they're awful. Students hate Curtin, and I don't blame them. He's lazy, and I don't think he bathes often enough."

Sally could have told Wynona that it was unprofessional of her to make derogatory comments about one of the school's instructors, but she knew Wynona wouldn't pay her any attention. And if she did pay attention, she wouldn't care. She was one of the people who actually ran the college, and if you crossed her, you could find yourself in deep trouble.

For example, Wynona put the final class schedule together each semester and got it ready for the print shop. While the department chairs made out the first draft and arranged for times and classrooms, Wynona had the power to make changes. Not in the times. Those were untouchable. But she could change the classroom assignments. Instructors who got on Wynona's bad side might discover that they had to walk quite a distance in the ten minutes between their nine and ten o'clock classes, for instance. The walk wasn't much of a nuisance on good days, but it could be quite unpleasant on a very hot one or on a day when the rain was falling in sheets and lightning tore across the skies while the wind turned umbrellas inside out. There were plenty of days like that near the Texas Gulf Coast.

So Sally just said, "I'd appreciate it if you'd give me a call when you find them."

"I'll do that," Wynona said, and Sally returned to her own office.

Wynona called around two o'clock, and Sally went to pick up the evaluations. When Sally walked into the office, Wynona was reading the students' comments. That, too, was unprofessional.

So was Wynona's appearance for that matter. She looked as if she should be working as a secretary in a disreputable auto repair shop instead of in the office of a college dean. She had big hair dyed a brassy color that had never been found in nature, she wore revealing blouses, and she had been known to talk a little trash from time to time. Sally didn't mind. She liked her, even though she wished Wynona would be a little more conventional now and then.

"These are just awful," Wynona said, looking up and flicking the forms with a red fingernail that seemed to Sally to be too long for doing any typing. "If anybody ever got canned around here, Curtin would be the guy. But nobody ever does. Get canned, I mean."

"Nobody?" Sally said as she reached across the desk and removed the green sheets of paper from Wynona's hand.

"Nobody. We had a guy working in the counseling center around five or six years ago. Jay Sammons. He had some kind of breakdown and started insulting the students instead of helping them. But did they fire him?" Wynona shook her head.

"*Nooooooo*. They put him in a little office way in the back of the center and had him doing enrollment statistics all day. He finally left when his wife got a job in San Antonio. Otherwise, he'd still be stuck back there, like that crazy old aunt in the attic that Ross Perot talked about."

Sally thanked Wynona for the evaluations and took them back to her office to look them over. They were no worse than the ones Curtin had received on the forms Sally had already seen. They were no better, either. Sally decided to call Curtin and have him come by for a conference to discuss his evaluations.

And that was when the trouble started.

3

"He always blamed you for his firing," Jack said. "I don't think he ever got over it."

"I'm sure he didn't," Sally said. She needed a Hershey bar, but she didn't want to show weakness in front of Jack. "And it was reasonable for him to blame me. After all, I was the one who made the recommendation."

"I know. I never thought it would really happen. He had tenure."

The Garden Gnome had had tenure, all right. Sally remembered that tenure was one of the first things he had mentioned when he came into her office on the day they were to discuss his evaluations.

"I don't really care what those things say," Curtin had told her, pointing to the incriminating sheets of paper on her desk. Sally had taken the time to clear a place for them, so they were right out in the open. "I have tenure, and no matter what a bunch of callow freshmen and sophomores say about me, I plan to continue teaching any way that I see fit."

Sally had looked him over. His beard was short, but it hadn't been trimmed for a while, and it appeared that part of his breakfast was caught in it. A bit of bacon, perhaps. His hair was no neater than his beard, although there wasn't any bacon in it that Sally could see. Curtin's face and eyes were red, and his shirt and pants were as wrinkled as if he'd slept in them for a week or so.

"I believe in academic freedom," he continued, sitting in the chair by her desk. "Don't you?"

"Of course I do," Sally told him. "I also believe that we have an obligation to give our students the education they're paying for."

Curtin put a hand to his mouth and belched, as if to show his opinion of that idea. The rest of the conversation was no more satisfactory, with Curtin hiding behind tenure and academic freedom as Sally pressed him to say he would take steps to become a more effective instructor.

"Who says I'm not effective? Those little twerps in my classes? Who are they to evaluate me? I have more college credits than any of them will ever get. They'll all be lucky if they don't spend their lives selling chalupas and burritos at the Speedy Taco."

"They're the ones we're paid to teach," Sally said, wondering if Curtin was entirely sane. "We have to give their opinions some weight."

"Maybe you do. I don't. Now if that's all you have to say, I have a class to teach."

"Go ahead, then. I'll call you soon about setting up some times for classroom observations."

Curtin had risen to his feet, but he sat back down, looking at Sally as if she had said something objectionable.

"Classroom evaluations?" he said. "What do you mean by that?"

"I mean exactly what I said. I'll be sitting in your classroom to observe your teaching methods and your interaction with the students. I'll let you pick the times and the classes so there won't be any surprises."

Curtin shook his head. "You aren't coming in my classroom."

"Yes," Sally said. "I am."

She dug through some of the papers on her desk and pulled out a copy of the college's evaluation policy. When she located the section she wanted, she started to read: "The department chair shall visit every instructor in his or her department at least once every two years and fill out the standard departmental observation form. The form is to be filed in the department chair's office after it has been discussed by the chair and the instructor and signed by both."

Curtin stared at her for a second. Then he said, "Barton didn't ever come in my classroom."

Sally had already checked the files Dr. Barton had left behind. As far as she could tell he hadn't done any classroom observations in the last ten years. Since the reports were supposed to have been kept on file in Barton's office, no one in the administration knew he hadn't been doing them. And the faculty certainly hadn't complained.

"I don't care what Dr. Barton did or didn't do," Sally said. She handed the policy manual to Curtin. "Here's the procedure, on page eighteen. You can read it for yourself."

Curtin didn't take the policy manual. He waved a hand at it to show what he thought of it, then stood up and said, "I don't care what that says. You're not coming in my classroom."

"Yes, I am," Sally said, and two weeks later, she did, though not at all in the way she had planned.

★ ★ ★

"I remember that little episode," Jack said when she reminded him of it. "That was the most excitement we'd had around here in a long time. Come to think of it, you've really livened things up since you became department chair. We've had much more exciting times since you came to good old HCC."

Having been thrown together with Jack during a couple of those exciting times, both of them involving murder, one of which Jack had been accused of committing, Sally had gotten to know him better than any other member of her faculty. She had been about to break her rule against dating members of the staff, but she had been saved from herself when he had become entangled, both figuratively and, Sally was certain, literally, with Vera Vaughn, who taught sociology and dressed like Ilsa, the She-Wolf of the SS. Jack was still a good friend, however, and Sally enjoyed his company.

"Did the Garden Gnome really hit that student with a stapler?" Jack asked. "Even for him, that was pretty drastic."

"He did it, though," Sally said. "I saw him."

She remembered the incident all too

well. She had been teaching her composition class, talking about thesis sentences, when she heard someone yelling. She thought at first that something was going on outside the building, but then she realized the noise was coming from the classroom across the hall from her own.

She knew that Curtin was teaching American literature in that room at that time, and she thought that maybe he was trying out some innovative method of getting his students' attention in order to improve his evaluations. She should have known better.

The yelling got louder, and Sally could hear two distinct voices, both of them angry. Her students heard them, too. Some of them looked a little apprehensive.

"Excuse me," Sally told the class. "I'll be right back."

She left her classroom and went across the hall. The door to Curtin's room was closed, but she could hear the yelling even more clearly now then before.

The door had a tall, narrow panel of glass on the left-hand side, and through it she could see Curtin standing beside his desk, toe to toe with a student who was considerably taller and brawnier. Their faces were red and their necks were swollen. It was clear to Sally that something bad was about to happen.

She could have gone for the campus police, as their office was in the same building, but she was afraid she'd be too late to stop the trouble. So she decided to intervene.

She was too late anyway.

She opened the door just as the student reached out with a big, beefy hand as if he might be going to take hold of Curtin's arm.

Curtin didn't give him a chance. There was a stapler sitting atop a stack of papers on the desk. Curtin grabbed the stapler and swung it, knocking the student's hand away.

Sally could have sworn that she heard a sharp hissing sound as every student in the classroom inhaled in shock.

The student was stunned. He looked down at his hand and then at Curtin.

"You hit me," he said.

Curtin was stunned, too. He had a disbelieving look on his face, as if he'd just awakened from what he'd thought was a nightmare and found it to be all too real. He dropped the stapler, and the sound it made when it hit the floor tiles echoed off the walls of the room.

Sally walked over to Curtin and said,

"Dismiss the class and stay here. I'll be back."

Then she told the student to come with her to the police office. He followed her in a daze, shaking his head. He kept saying, "He hit me," over and over.

"Whatever happened to that kid?" Jack asked.

"Jerry," Sally said. "Jerry Ketchum."

"Right. Whatever happened to him?"

"You mean officially?"

"Yeah."

"Nothing. He was out of line. He admitted as much. He'd been upset with the grade on a test he'd taken, not to mention that Curtin hadn't put a single mark on it to show how he arrived at the grade. So he'd protested. Curtin argued with him, and things got heated."

"They sure did. What happened to Ketchum unofficially?"

"He dropped the class after we got a replacement for Curtin, and I don't know what happened to him after that. I don't recall ever seeing his name on a graduation list. Maybe he dropped out of school altogether, or maybe he transferred to another college. It could be that he blamed himself a little for what happened."

"Well, it does sound as if he got a little carried away."

"Yes. But that was nothing compared to what Curtin did. You can't hit a student. You can yell at him, maybe even call him names, but you can't hit him."

"Curtin claimed it was self-defense."

"The student was reaching out, but he wasn't really threatening Curtin. Curtin overreacted."

"Didn't Ketchum's parents threaten to sue the college?"

"Yes, but since Ketchum more or less admitted that he'd started the whole uproar, they decided not to sue. I don't think they'd have been successful."

"They thought you should have done more, didn't they?"

"Yes. They thought we were all too easy on Curtin, but their son shared some of the blame. They didn't like my saying that, but it was true."

"There was a little more to it than that, though."

"There certainly was. Curtin had been drinking. I could smell liquor when I stood next to him. He never admitted it, and of course I couldn't prove it, but it was obvious."

"And so he got fired."

"That's right. I don't think a faculty member at HCC had ever been fired before."

"And it was all because of you."

"Me?" Sally said. "How could it have been because of me? I didn't hit anybody with a stapler. I didn't come to class drunk at ten in the morning."

"Curtin claimed he wasn't drunk."

"All right. I'll give him that much. He wasn't actually drunk. But he'd been drinking."

"He didn't take any Breathalyzer tests."

"You sound like his lawyer."

"I'm just saying what he said. And he believed it. Therefore, it was all your fault."

"It wasn't my fault. And the school was very generous with him. In fact, the college gave him a sizable severance package just to get rid of him."

"That's right," Jack said, "and he invested most of it in tech stocks. He was riding high there for a while."

Sally knew that part of the story, too. Curtin had let several of his former colleagues know how well he was doing and how stupid they were for continuing to work while he lived a life of ease and tranquility.

"It didn't last," Sally said.

"Tell me about it. I had some of my retirement funds invested in tech stocks, too, I'm sorry to say. I didn't lose as much as Curtin, but I lost plenty. Curtin blamed you for that, too."

"He blamed me for the tech stock debacle? That's pushing it, even for Curtin."

"Well, he didn't actually think you caused the collapse of the NASDAQ. But he blamed you for the fact that he was forced into retirement, so it follows that he blamed you for the fact that since the market dropped, he'd been living somewhere around the poverty line. I'm surprised that Fieldstone hasn't called you in for a little talk about it."

"He's called me in, but not to talk about Curtin. He wants me to repudiate witchcraft."

Jack laughed so hard that Sally was afraid he might fall off the chair. When he finally got control of himself again, he said, "I got that e-mail. The more I thought about it, the more I thought it made sense. It explains that cat of yours, for one thing."

"Lola is not a witch's familiar."

"She's mean enough to be."

Sally knew that Jack was only joking, but she still felt a bit defensive. She didn't like for people to say bad things about Lola. It was all right for Sally to say them, but others weren't allowed.

"Lola's a very sweet cat," Sally said.

"To you, maybe. Not to anybody else."

"Let's get back to Fieldstone," Sally said.

Jack wiped his eyes. "Yeah. I thought he might call you in to talk to you about Curtin."

"What happened with Curtin was a long time ago. We've said all that had to be said, held all the hearings, and closed the book on the whole mess. His death doesn't change that."

"The book wasn't closed on everything. Not for Curtin."

"What else is there?"

"The bond issue. Curtin was working behind the scenes to get the bond defeated. Have you seen those ads paid for by the Citizens for Fiscal Responsibility?"

Sally had seen them. The position taken by the ad writer was that the college had been spending money foolishly for years. There was no need for a bond issue, just a change in administration. Throw the rascals (meaning the president and the board) out, hire a new president and vote in new board members with a vision for the future, a vision that didn't involve bond issues and more taxes.

"Curtin had something to do with the ads," Jack said. "He planned to run for the board at the next election, and then you'd be toast. Along with everyone else who got him fired."

"I didn't get him fired. He got himself fired."

"Tell that to Curtin."

"I can't," Sally said. "According to you, he's dead."

"Yeah. That's probably your fault, too."

"He might think so if he were around to offer an opinion." Sally knew that sounded cold, but she had never liked Curtin, and it was hard to feel sorry for him now that he was gone. "How did he die?"

"That's an interesting question," Jack said. "The rumor is that he choked to death on his own blood."

Arrest Warrant for Sarah Good, February 1692

Whereas Mrs. Joseph Hutcheson, Thomas Putnam, Edward Putnam, and Thomas Preston, Yeomen of Salem Village in the County of Essex personally appeared before us, and made complaint on behalf of their Majesties against Sarah Good, the wife of William Good of Salem Village, abovesaid for suspicion of witchcraft by her committed, and thereby much injury done to Elizabeth Parris, Abigail Williams, Anna Putnam, and Elizabeth Hubert, all of Salem Village aforesaid sundry times within this two months and lately also done, at Salem Village contrary to the peace of our Sover'n L'd and Lady W'm & Mary King & Queen of Engld &c — You are therefore in their Majesties' names hereby required to apprehend & bring before us the said Sarah Good, tomorrow about ten of the clock in the forenoon at the house of Lt. Nathaniell Ingersalls in Salem Village or as soon as may be then & there to be Examined Relating to the abovesaid premises, and hereof you are not to fail at your peril.

4

Jack Neville walked down the hallway to his office, glad that Sally hadn't asked him how he knew so much about what the Garden Gnome had been thinking.

The truth was that Curtin, for reasons that Jack couldn't fathom, had gotten the idea that Jack was his friend. Maybe it was because they'd taught in the same department for years, often in adjoining classrooms, though they'd hardly ever spoken more than a couple of words to each other.

But since the tech stock debacle, Curtin had called Jack every now and then to tell him the latest chapter of his sad story or to complain about how badly HCC in general — and Sally Good in particular — had treated him.

For reasons he couldn't explain, Jack had always listened patiently. He told himself that it was doing Curtin good to get the bile out of his system, and it was better for him to be taking it out on Jack than on someone else. Sally, for example.

Besides, Jack was interested when Curtin started telling him about his plans to run for the college board. Jack didn't think the man had a chance of winning, but if he did, things would certainly be different. The current board was composed entirely of people who had the school's best interests in mind. Curtin would be a loose cannon, and he could cause a lot of trouble.

When Jack had received the e-mail about Sally's being a witch, his first thought was that Curtin had sent it. And maybe he had. Jack didn't know when he had died. He could have sent the e-mail first. The e-mail had come from some Web address of convenience, and it could have been sent by anyone.

At any rate, Jack didn't want to think about it. He had other things on his mind, like his new computer game addiction. It seemed that every time he managed to conquer one addiction, a new one took its place. So, he thought, he probably didn't really conquer anything. He just replaced one addiction with another. This time, while kicking the Free Cell habit, he had become addicted to Spider Solitaire. He was just advancing to the second level, and he was eager to try his hand at a few games before his next class. He looked at his watch. Ten-thirty. He had half an hour.

Except that he had company. Like Sally, and most of the other faculty members, Jack rarely locked his office, and he often left the door open all day, even while teaching or visiting someone else's office. Students at HCC were honest. Either that, or they didn't want anything he owned. He'd never had anything stolen.

But now and then unexpected guests turned up. Sometimes the guests were a pleasant surprise. Sometimes they weren't. In this case, Eric Desmond, chief of the HCC police, and Detective Weems of the local police force were waiting for him.

Jack felt an unpleasant sense of déjà vu. It hadn't been so very long ago that he'd been accused of murder, hauled off to the police station, and given the third degree.

"Not again," he said, looking at the two men who were making themselves at home in his office.

"Don't worry, Neville," Desmond said. "This isn't about you. Nothing to get excited about."

Desmond was nearly sixty, but he was fit and trim and looked like a much younger man. And he dressed like one, too. It was hard for Jack to think of a policeman as being dapper, but if there was ever a dapper cop, Desmond was the one.

"I'm not excited," Jack said. "Just scared of getting the third degree again."

"We didn't give you the third degree," Weems said. "If we had, your kneecaps wouldn't have healed by now."

Weems wasn't dapper. He was, in fact, a little bit sloppy. He was tall, with a big stomach. Jack thought he could have used some diet and fitness advice from Desmond.

"You're joking, right?" Jack said.

Weems gave him a flat stare. "You don't want to know."

He was right, even if he was only kidding, so Jack just nodded.

"What's all this?" Weems asked, indicating a stack of books on Jack's desk beside his computer. "I thought you'd be reading Hemingway or somebody like that."

The books were all histories of rock 'n' roll, as that was one of Jack's interests. Community college instructors weren't required to publish, but if they did, the publications didn't affect their pay or their status. Jack liked to write, and the school's attitude gave him the freedom to write about whatever he enjoyed. At the mo-

45

ment, he was working on an article about independent recording labels in Texas in the late 1950s, like the "D" label on which the Big Bopper had originally recorded "Chantilly Lace" in 1958.

Jack liked the fifties. He'd seen *Rebel Without a Cause* on television at an impressionable age and loved everything about it: the cars, the clothes, the actors, the attitudes. Since that time he'd studied the era, especially its music, with something bordering on obsession. But he never let his infatuation with the past interfere with his life in the present.

"I'm interested in history," Jack said in answer to Weems's question. "You haven't said why you're here."

"Because a friend of yours died," Weems said. "Harold Curtin."

The building was air-conditioned, but Jack started to sweat a little. He didn't like the way the conversation was going.

"I heard about that. But Harold wasn't my friend."

"He had your telephone number written in a notebook by his phone. He must have talked to you recently."

"He called now and then. Not recently. Why do you care?"

"Did you hear how he died?"

"Some kind of hemorrhage," Jack said. "Why would that interest the police?"

"We're always interested when someone dies under odd circumstances."

Jack wondered what the odd circumstances could be. He'd heard about Curtin's death from Troy Beauchamp, who was always the first with the news about anything and everything. Troy had been on his way to class when he'd told Jack, and he hadn't mentioned any odd circumstances. He'd made Jack promise not to tell Sally. Troy wanted to tell her himself, but he didn't have time before class. Jack had promised, but he'd kept his fingers crossed.

"I didn't hear anything about the circumstances," Jack said. "Just that he died of a hemorrhage."

"You know anything about an e-mail that was sent out about your department head?" Weems asked.

"If you mean the one about her being a witch, I got a copy. So did a lot of other people, or so I've heard. What does that have to do with Curtin?"

"Maybe nothing. What did he call you about?"

"Just to complain about life in general. We taught in the same department for a

47

long time so we knew each other. I think he needed to vent now and then, and I'm sure I wasn't the only one he called."

"Did he ever mention being cursed?"

Jack almost laughed, but Weems wasn't the kind of guy you laughed at. Jack stopped himself just in time and said, "No, I don't think he ever said anything about being cursed. Was he?"

"I don't believe in things like that," Weems said. "But Curtin might have. Do you know much about the Bible?"

Jack looked at Desmond, who hadn't said a word since Weems had begun talking. Desmond just shrugged. Jack turned back to Weems and said, "I took some courses in biblical history in college. I'm far from an expert. What does the Bible have to do with anything?"

"There's a verse in the book of Revelations," Weems said.

"Revelation," Jack said, remembering that Sally had told him once that Roy Don Talon, one of the school's board members, had made the same mistake. "There's no s on it. It's 'the Revelation of St. John the Divine.' "

It was Weems's turn to look at Desmond, who shrugged again.

"You learn something every day," Weems

said. "Anyway, there's a verse in the book of Revela*tion* that says, 'For men have shed the blood of saints and prophets, and thou hast given them blood to drink. It is their due.' "

"I'll take your word for it," Jack said. "I don't remember that verse. And I'm not quite sure what point you're trying to make."

Weems didn't look up from his notebook, and he didn't respond to Jack's comment. He said, "And then there's something from somewhere else. 'God will give you blood to drink.' " He looked up at Jack. "Ever hear that one?"

"I've seen it in a couple of places," Jack said.

"What places?"

"It's in a book by Nathaniel Hawthorne, *The House of the Seven Gables*, and it's in the records of the Salem witchcraft trials."

"You know who said it at those trials?"

Jack knew. He'd studied the trials in graduate school, and the e-mail about Sally had brought the name back to mind.

"A woman named Sarah Good," he said.

Weems looked at his notebook, nodded, and flipped the notebook closed. He stuck the notebook back in his pocket.

"I guess that's it, then."

He stood up, and Desmond opened the office door. The two cops went out. Desmond nodded at Jack as he left, but Weems ignored him. However, before they'd gone more than a couple of steps, Weems turned back to Jack.

"I just thought of another question," Weems said.

Jack wondered if Weems had been watching *Columbo* reruns.

"What?" he said.

"Did Dr. Good and Curtin have any problems?"

Jack hoped that Weems couldn't tell how much he was sweating now. He said, "There was an incident once. Chief Desmond can tell you more about that than I could."

"I wasn't talking about the past. I was talking about lately."

"Not that I know about," Jack said.

"No conflict about the current interests of the college?"

Jack could have said, "That makes two questions," but he didn't think Weems would appreciate the humor. So instead he said, "I don't have any idea about that."

"How about the bond election?"

That's three, Jack thought. He said, "They were on opposite sides."

"That's what I thought," Weems said.

He seemed about to say more, but the bell rang and students flooded into the hallway chattering away to each other and into their cell phones. Weems gave Jack a little wave and turned to join Desmond, who was waiting for him. Jack watched them go. He was sure they were headed for Sally's office, but he didn't follow them. He knew they wouldn't like that one bit, and he had a class in a few minutes. He turned to his desk and started getting his things together.

5

Troy Beauchamp made a beeline for Sally's office as soon as class was over. He didn't actually shove any of the milling students aside, but he did brush a few of them with his shoulders as he dashed down the hallway. He arrived at Sally's door practically breathless, but he still had enough air left to say, "Have you heard about Harold Curtin?" as soon as he reached the doorway.

Sally looked up from the papers she'd been grading and smiled. She knew Troy was going to be crushed, but she told him the truth.

"Yes," she said. "Jack told me."

Troy was rendered momentarily speechless, which was for him an unaccustomed condition. He was a careless dresser, and as he stood there with his mouth slightly agape, Sally noticed that he'd missed a loop when he put on his belt. She didn't tell him, however.

"Neville's a rat," Troy said after a few

seconds. He ran a hand through his already tousled hair. "He promised he'd let me tell you. It's a shame when you can't even trust your own colleagues."

Sally smiled, but the smile slipped away when Weems and Desmond appeared behind Beauchamp.

Troy turned around to see what Sally was looking at. When he saw the two policemen standing at his back, he said, "Excuse me," and left without another word.

Knowing Troy as she did, Sally would have been willing to bet that Troy hadn't gone far. He was most likely lurking somewhere within earshot, so she invited Weems and Desmond to come into her office.

"You don't have to close the door if you just need my help in how to use *who* and *whom* correctly," Sally said. "Or even if you just want to know something about the use of the apostrophe."

Weems and Desmond stepped inside, and Desmond closed the door behind them. The door wasn't an entirely effective barrier, because it had louvers in it, but it was better than nothing. If Troy overheard anything they said, it would be all over the building within minutes, if not seconds.

"I take it you aren't here to get any information about errors in writing," Sally said. "You might as well have a seat, then."

Weems sat in the chair beside her desk, while Desmond took one at the computer desk behind her. Sally waited patiently for them to tell her what they wanted.

"We've been talking to Jack Neville," Weems said after a second or two.

Sally thought he would go on, but he didn't. So she asked how Jack was doing, as if she didn't know.

"He's all right," Weems said. "He wasn't very helpful, though."

Sally hadn't eaten a Hershey bar after Jack had left her office, but now she wished she had. Digesting chocolate would have helped her deal with Weems.

"What kind of help do you need?" she asked. "Is it about Jack?"

"It's not about Neville this time. I'm looking for some information about one of your former teachers."

"Which one?" Sally asked, though she was pretty sure she knew the answer.

"Harold Curtin," Weems said, confirming her suspicions. "You and he had some problems at one time, I think."

"One problem, and it was his, not mine.

It was handled by the college. I haven't seen him since he retired."

"Retired?" Weems gave her a skeptical look. "I guess that's one way to put it. But he didn't leave voluntarily, did he?"

"He didn't have much choice in the matter, if that's what you mean."

"That's what I mean," Weems said. "And now he's dead. You've heard about that?"

"I've heard."

"News gets around this place fast," Weems said with a glance at Desmond.

"Telegraph, telephone, tell a teacher," Desmond said. He seemed a bit nervous to Sally, and that was unusual. Desmond wasn't the nervous sort. "The three fastest means of communication in higher education. Not necessarily in that order, either."

"That's a really old joke," Weems said. "Does anybody these days even know what *telegraph* means?"

"I know," Desmond told him. "But then I'm an old guy."

"I guess so." Weems turned back to Sally. "You're probably wondering why I'm asking you these questions."

"That's right. But I assume you're planning to tell me sooner or later."

"Sooner," Weems said. "There's a possibility that Curtin was murdered."

Sally sank back in her chair. That was one thing she hadn't expected to hear.

"Who did it?" she asked.

"If I knew that," Weems said, "I wouldn't be here now."

Sally had been afraid he was going to tell her something like that.

"Surely you don't think I had anything to do with it."

Weems didn't answer the question. He said, "I don't have any writing questions, but I have a biblical one. It's about a verse from St. John's Revelation."

Sally recognized the verse, and of course she knew the source of the next quotation that he asked her about.

"What does that have to do with Harold Curtin?" she wanted to know.

"Because we found both these verses near his body. And your name was signed to them."

Sally said she found that hard to believe, and she asked if Weems wanted a handwriting sample.

"Well, it wasn't exactly your name. It was a name a lot like yours."

"Sarah Good," Sally said.

"How did you know that?"

56

"I've read about the witchcraft trials, and Sarah's name has been brought to my attention lately."

"By an e-mail," Weems said.

Sally wondered if everyone in town had gotten that crazy e-mail.

"Somebody doesn't like me very much," she said.

"Somebody liked Curtin even less," Desmond pointed out. Sally had almost forgotten he was in the room.

"Has anyone been trying to find out who sent that e-mail?" Sally asked him.

"Yes," Desmond said. "We have some of the computer guys working on it. They tell me it was sent from an 'alias,' whatever that means, and that it will have to be tracked back through a whole series of aliases. They might be able to do it, or they might not."

"It mentioned Sarah Good," Sally said. "So there might be some connection between it and those notes at Harold's place. But the notes don't mean he was murdered. He might have written them himself."

"We're checking on that," Weems told her. "We're also checking on his medical history. We'll know a lot more by the end of the day."

Sally's telephone rang. The call was from Fieldstone's secretary, Eva Dillon, who told Sally that Fieldstone wanted to see her in his office immediately if not sooner.

"Roy Don Talon is in the office with him," Eva said.

It required a mighty effort, but Sally didn't moan. She told Eva that she would be there as soon as she could.

"That was the president's office," she told Weems. "Dr. Fieldstone wants to see me."

"We're about through here, anyway," Weems said. "I just wanted to let you know what's going on. Sort of a friendly warning, you might say."

Sally didn't think of Weems as friendly in the least. She thought he had other reasons for his visit. After all, she'd been involved in a couple of his cases before, and she couldn't blame him for checking on her. The e-mail was bad enough, and all those references to Sarah Good lying around Harold Curtin's place didn't help. However, she didn't have time to worry about things like that at the moment. She was using all her worry muscles on Roy Don Talon.

Weems and Desmond left, and Sally opened the bottom drawer of her desk.

That was where she kept the Hershey bars. She wasn't going to face Talon without eating one.

From the Examination of Sarah Good

Judge Hathorne: *"Sarah Good what evil spirit have you familiarity with?"*

Sarah Good: *"None."*

Judge Hathorne: *"Have you made no contract with the devil?"*

Sarah Good: *"No."*

Judge Hathorne: *"Why do you hurt these children?"*

Sarah Good: *"I do not hurt them. I scorn it."*

Judge Hathorne: *"Who do you employ then to do it?"*

Sarah Good: *"I employ nobody."*

Judge Hathorne: *"What creature do you employ then?"*

Sarah Good: *"No creature, but I am falsely accused."*

6

Roy Don Talon was a member of the college board of trustees, and he was not fond of Sally. He'd been involved with the "satanic painting" episode that Fieldstone had mentioned earlier, and that hadn't endeared Sally to him. Later on, he'd been even more involved in an incident that had almost landed him in jail. He'd escaped imprisonment because he had no knowledge of certain goings-on at his car dealership, but it had been a near thing, and he blamed Sally for his close call.

Eva Dillon greeted Sally in the outer office and asked if she could use a Snickers.

Sally thanked her and told her that she'd already had a Hershey.

"Good," Eva said. "Nobody should have to deal with Roy Don Talon without a good chocolate buzz."

She ushered Sally into Fieldstone's office, where Talon and the president were waiting for her. In contrast to Fieldstone, who was dressed impeccably in a navy blue suit, starched white shirt, and navy tie, Talon might have been on his way to attend a rodeo or a Dixie Chicks concert. He wore a brown western-cut suit and brown boots. His string tie was also brown, and his silver belt buckle looked like the headlight of an oncoming locomotive.

Sally wasn't sure whether Talon dressed as he did because he'd been a lifelong fan of country-and-western music in general and Porter Waggoner in particular or because he was a shrewd salesman. He had one of the largest automobile dealerships in the Houston area, and his television ads, which turned up at all hours on most of the cable channels as well as the local stations, played up western themes. In the latest, Talon was depicted riding a mechanical bull in the middle of his car lot, hanging on with one hand as he waved his ten-gallon Stetson in the air with the other. After the ride, he slid off the bull and announced that "We won't give you any bull at Talon Auto!"

If that was true, and Sally didn't believe it for a second, there was still plenty of bull to go around when Roy Don met people personally.

"Howdy," Roy Don said, standing up when Sally entered the room.

He extended a cool hand to her, and she shook it because he expected her to. She was glad he didn't try to hug her.

"Have a seat, Dr. Good," Fieldstone said. He was behind his desk and didn't join in the handshaking ritual. "Mr. Talon wants to talk to us about some concerns he has."

"That's the plain truth," Talon said. He sat down, holding his cowboy hat on his lap. "I do have me some concerns."

Sally sat on the couch and waited for him to tell her what the concerns were, even though she had a pretty good idea.

"I got an e-mail this mornin'," Talon said, looking at her. He had a deep, sincere voice, which was good for his television ads and probably didn't hurt when he was closing a business deal. "It was about you, Dr. Good."

"I think a lot of people got that e-mail," Sally said.

"Yeah, so do I, and that's the problem. We can't have people here in Hughes thinkin' we got us a witch on our staff here at the college. That's not good for our image in the community. People might start rememberin' that incident we had here with that satanic paintin'."

It took an effort, but Sally refrained from

sighing. She said, "It wasn't a satanic painting. It was just a picture of a goat."

"Yeah, well, that's your story, and I don't blame you for stickin' to it. But it all seems to me to fit together."

"I don't know what you mean."

"Sure you do. Witchcraft and satanism and all those things like that. They're just one and the same, and now you're mixed up with both of 'em."

Sally looked at Fieldstone, who at least had the grace to avert his eyes. She knew he couldn't call a board member an idiot, but she wished he'd stick up for his faculty. Not that she really expected him to in this case, as he'd already told her pretty much the same thing himself.

"Mr. Talon," she said, "do you really believe in witches?"

"Well now, of course I do. It talks about 'em in the Bible, and I believe every word in there, and that includes the maps. But maybe you don't feel the same way."

Sally wasn't going to fall into that trap. She knew better than to argue about religion with someone like Roy Don Talon.

"I should have asked if you believe that *I'm* a witch," she said.

Talon moved his hat around on his lap and shifted a little in the chair.

"Well now, I can't say about that. I know that sometimes an e-mail might not be true."

"Let's say I am a witch. That would mean I could cast a spell on you right now. I could turn you into a cat, or maybe a pig."

Not that I'd have to work very hard on that last one, Sally thought.

Fieldstone cleared his throat, but Sally didn't look in his direction.

"Or I could put a hex on your car dealership," she said to Talon. "I could cause your sales to drop to nothing."

Fieldstone cleared his throat more loudly, and Sally turned toward him.

"Do you need a drink of water?" she asked.

Fieldstone glared at her. "No. I'm fine."

"I thought maybe you had a sore throat, or a cough."

"No. It's nothing."

Fieldstone's face was getting red, but Sally didn't care.

"I'm glad. Are you sure you don't want to get a drink?"

"I don't need a drink." Fieldstone's voice was strained. "I just need for you and Mr. Talon to start talking sensibly. He knows you're not going to put a spell on him."

"I'm not so sure of that," Sally said. "What about it, Mr. Talon?"

Talon wouldn't look directly at her.

"I guess I hope you wouldn't," he said.

"Good grief," Sally said. "Look, Mr. Talon, I happen to have the same last name as a witch who was executed over three hundred years ago because that was my husband's name. Not mine. I should never have taken it when I married him."

Talon looked as shocked at Sally's last statement as he might have if Sally had produced a broom out of thin air, mounted it, and flown around the room.

"There's no call to get radical," he said.

"I'm not getting radical, but I am getting a little tired of this witchcraft business. I'm not a witch, I don't know any witches, and I'm not going to say anything more about it."

"Well, see, I wouldn't say any more, myself, but it's just that there's already been some talk around town, what with poor Harold Curtin dyin' the way he did and all. You did know about that, didn't you?"

"I heard about it, and I'm very sorry. I don't see what it has to do with me, however."

Sally certainly wasn't going to mention her little visit with Weems, and she didn't think either Talon or Fieldstone would have heard about it. Not yet, anyway.

"I guess it might not have anything to do with you," Talon said, "but I got a call from Sherm Jackson this mornin'. I think you've met his wife."

Sally had met Jennifer Jackson, all right. She was the leader of a group called Mothers Against Witchcraft, the group that had tried to get the Harry Potter books banned from the Hughes Public Library. She and Sally had developed an intense case of mutual dislike.

"I've met her," Sally said.

"Then you know how she is. Sherm said she wanted me to set up a meetin' for her with Dr. Fieldstone, and I just thought we'd better get a few things settled first."

"Like what?"

"She wants you to be at the meetin'. I think maybe she has it in her head to get you fired."

"And what do you have in your head?" Sally asked.

"Me?" Talon fidgeted as if he thought Sally might put that hex on him if he said the wrong thing. "Not a thing."

Sally could see the headline now: DOCTORS EXAMINE TALON'S HEAD, FIND NOTHING.

"I just thought you should know what you're in for," Talon said. "That's all. I'm just the messenger."

"It seems to me that just a little while ago you were awfully concerned about that e-mail."

"Not me. I was just sayin' how it put me in mind of that satanic picture."

Sally didn't want to get started on that topic again. She looked at Fieldstone.

"Have you set up the meeting already?"

Fieldstone opened the middle drawer of his desk and took out a piece of paper. He pretended to be looking at it, but Sally knew the paper was just an excuse for him to avoid her eyes.

"I had Eva check your schedule," Fieldstone said. "You don't have a nine-thirty class on Tuesdays, and Mrs. Jackson is free then, too. So we'll meet here in my office tomorrow morning."

Sally stood up. She looked first at Talon and then at Fieldstone. Talon looked at his hat, while Fieldstone continued to look at the piece of paper he was holding.

"I'll be here," Sally said.

7

Whenever Sally felt especially frustrated, she liked to go to the college firing range and run a few rounds through the barrel of her Ladysmith. So after leaving Fieldstone's office she went straight home and got out her pistol.

She had recently bought a new sidearm. Her first pistol had been a Ladysmith .38 caliber revolver, the Model 36, but she had sold that one and bought a new 9mm automatic that held nine cartridges if she wanted to keep one in the chamber, which she didn't. She figured eight shots would be enough for any villain she was likely to encounter in Hughes, Texas.

When she bought the new pistol, she also purchased a gun safe. She had always kept the revolver in the lingerie drawer of her dresser, but she had decided that wasn't a very smart thing to do. It wasn't that she thought Lola might get hold of the gun and do damage to herself or someone else. Lola was just a cat, but she knew better than to fool around with guns and Sally didn't worry about her. Because Hughes was so close to Houston and often afflicted with big-city crimes, Sally was more worried about theft than she was about Lola misusing a firearm.

The gun safe was mounted on a shelf of Sally's bedroom closet. When she went into the room, she saw Lola lying on the bed. She was stretched out, half on her back and half on her side.

"Very ladylike," Sally said.

Lola rolled onto her stomach and looked at Sally and said, "Meow," which was about the extent of her vocabulary. She could, however, invest the sound with a multiplicity of meanings.

Sally opened the closet door, moved aside some dresses that were hanging on the bar, and revealed the cast aluminum and steel gun safe. She punched in the combination on the keypad, and the safe came open, presenting the internal holster.

Sally took out the automatic and carried it to her dresser. She still kept the cartridges in the lingerie drawer, separate from the pistol. She didn't like to leave them in the clip, as she thought that might damage the spring. And besides, she wasn't fond of having a loaded weapon in the house, even if Lola knew better than to use it.

The leather pistol case was also in the drawer. Sally put the pistol in it and zipped it. Then she put a box of cartridges in her purse.

Lola watched these preparations with a look of complete indifference, but then that was the look she usually wore. She would have looked the same if Sally had danced around the room in toe shoes and a tutu.

Sally sat on the bed beside Lola, who was a calico cat, and from time to time a bit of a pain. Sally had heard that calicos were a temperamental sort. Today, however, Lola seemed in a very relaxed mood. Sally rubbed her head. Lola stuck out her chin, flattened her ears, and purred.

"I know you're the meanest cat west of the Mississippi," Sally told her, thinking of what Jack had said. "But I'm not going to let anyone accuse you of being a witch's familiar."

Lola continued to purr as if she didn't care what anyone called her as long as she got plenty of attention.

"How about a kitty treat?" Sally said, standing up.

Lola jumped to the floor and trotted off to the kitchen, where her food bowl was located. Sally got the treats out of the cabinet. They were supposed to be good for Lola's teeth, so Sally put two of them in the bowl. Lola inhaled them and looked up expectantly.

"You're supposed to chew them," Sally said. "They're not going to do any tartar removal if you swallow them whole."

"Meow," Lola said.

"You've had two," Sally said. "That's all you get."

"Meow?"

"No, you're not too fat. You're just . . . pleasingly plump. But you can't have any more treats today. Why don't you go play with your catnip mouse while I go to the firing range."

"Meow," Lola said, and she stalked out of the kitchen, her tail sticking straight up in the air.

Sally watched her go and then glanced over at the answering machine. The red light was blinking, so Sally stepped to where she could see the caller ID. There was only one call, and it was from her mother. Sally loved her mother, but she didn't feel like having a conversation with her at the moment, so she ignored the blinking light and took her pistol out to her Acura.

She put the gun in the trunk. She was licensed to carry a concealed handgun, but she didn't like to have the pistol in the car with her. Another meaningless safety precaution, perhaps, but she felt better when the gun was stowed away. Of course if someone decided to carjack her, she was going to be sorry the Ladysmith wasn't on the seat beside her.

As she drove to the firing range, Sally reflected that most people, at least those given to stereotyping, would be unlikely to suspect an English teacher, especially a woman, of being a firearms enthusiast. And Sally had never expected to become one. She had taken the college's concealed handgun course more or less as a lark and discovered that she had an affinity for pistols. She liked the craft that went into their workmanship, and she liked the heft of them in her hand. She didn't plan to become a part of a well-regulated militia, but she didn't plan to give up her gun, either.

She had also discovered that she was a pretty good marksperson. No one had to teach her how to shoot. It just seemed to come naturally to her. She liked the feeling of competence that a tight grouping of shots gave her.

She checked in at the range, glad to see that no one else was there to practice at that time of the afternoon. She put on the ear protectors, then loaded the Ladysmith's clip. After placing the clip in the pistol, she took a deep breath and took the pistol in a two-handed grip. She let her breath out slowly as she sighted in on the paper target with both eyes open. When she felt as relaxed as she was going to get, she pulled the trigger. The target jumped, and she fired again. And then again, until she had fired eight times.

The figure on the target was that of a heavyset man wearing a hat. Sally paused to reload as the target moved toward her, wondering how long it had been since she'd actually seen a man wearing a dress hat. Her conclusion was that it had been a long time.

When she inspected the target, Sally wasn't pleased with the grouping. Her shots had been all over the place, proving that she was still upset from her visit with Fieldstone and Talon. She'd thought maybe her quiet time with Lola had helped calm her down, but she'd been wrong. She signaled for the target to be moved out again, this time to fifteen yards. She was confident that she could do better even at the greater distance.

She was right. When she inspected the target again, she had a nice tight group in the crudely drawn figure's chest. She smiled and settled down to do some more shooting.

Leaving the firing range, Sally was taken aback by the stifling humidity outside. The range was air-conditioned and quite cool, but there had been a brief rain shower while Sally was in the building, and breathing was like sucking air through a steamed towel.

The hot and humid air wasn't doing much for Sally's hair, either. She often thought that women in dry climates didn't really know what a bad hair day was. Living near the Gulf Coast, Sally was guaranteed at least three hundred and fifty bad hair days a year.

She locked the pistol in the trunk of her car, feeling pretty good about just about everything except her hair. The e-mail that had been sent out was, she felt certain, nothing more than a prank perpetrated by some student who was unhappy with a grade. Probably it had been sent by someone in her American literature class, since they were the ones who'd most recently been discussing witchcraft. Sally thought immediately of Wayne Compton, but she knew it couldn't have been Wayne. He was kind of a pest, but he didn't have a malicious bone in his body. She was going through a mental list of the other students as she got behind the wheel of the Acura, oblivious of anything going on around her, which explained why she jumped and banged her head on the roof when a loud horn sounded nearby.

Sally rubbed her head, further frizzing her hair, and looked around. A black Lincoln Navigator was pulling to a stop beside her. Vera Vaughn was the only faculty member who had a Navigator. It wouldn't have been out of character for her to own something even bigger, like a Hummer, though Sally thought that even a Hummer might not have ten cup holders. But the Navigator did. Sally had counted them once.

The passenger-side window of the Navigator slid down, and Jack Neville leaned out.

"We tried to call you," he said, "but you must have your cell phone turned off."

Sally seldom turned on her cell phone,

and certainly never in the firing range, where she didn't like distractions.

"I thought you might be here taking out your frustrations," Jack said, "considering the kind of day you must have had."

Sally thought that Jack knew her better than just about anyone at HCC. She wasn't sure that was a good thing.

"Vera and I would like to talk to you," Jack went on. "If you have time."

"Right now?" Sally said.

"Now, but not here. We could meet you somewhere. How about the Adobe Hacienda? We could have a margarita."

Sally checked her watch. It was five-thirty, not too early for a margarita, and she wouldn't mind having Mexican food for dinner later.

"All right," she said. "I'll meet you there."

The window slid up and the Navigator made its way out of the parking lot. Wondering what Vera and Jack had to say, Sally followed them.

8

Sally was pretty sure that the Adobe Hacienda wasn't made of adobe. For that matter, it wasn't a hacienda. It was just a Mexican restaurant on the outskirts of Hughes, built to look as if it might be made of adobe and as if it might not have been out of place on a large ranch somewhere in Mexico.

Sally didn't know if it really resembled a hacienda, as she had never been to a ranch in Mexico. She did know that the margaritas were good and that the food was even better.

When she arrived at the parking lot, Vera and Jack were standing beside the Navigator waiting for her. Vera, looking less like one of the Valkyrie than usual, was dressed modestly in jeans, a plaid shirt, and high-heeled boots.

Sally was wearing the same Kaspar pantsuit that she had worn to school that morning. "Inexpensive, but nice," was what her mother had always said about the clothing line that Sally favored. Sally didn't think the pantsuit had been all that inexpensive, but she'd gotten it on sale, and it didn't pay to argue with her mother.

Jack and Vera waved to Sally, and she joined them. Heat waves shimmered up off the asphalt.

"Let's go in," Jack said. "It's too hot to stand out here."

They went inside, with Jack allowing Vera to open the door. Vera was a militant feminist, and Sally knew that she didn't like to have men opening doors for her.

It was cool inside the restaurant, and the smell of sizzling fajitas filled the entryway. The walls of the restaurant were decorated with colorful serapes and sombreros. Crossed maracas hung beside them, and piñatas dangled from the ceiling. Sally had often wondered if there was anything inside the piñatas, but she'd never been quite curious enough to whack one with a stick and find out. Maybe if she had enough margaritas some night, she'd give it a try.

There was music playing over hidden speakers, and although Sally hadn't taken Spanish since college, she could understand some of the words: *lágrimas,* for one. *Corazón* was another.

Vera asked for a back booth, and as they were following the server to it, Sally saw that Jorge Rodriguez and Mae Wilkins were seated at a table on the opposite side of the room. If she hadn't been wondering about what Vera and Jack wanted, Sally thought, she might have noticed Jorge's car outside. There had been a bit of chemistry between her and Jorge, and she had thought that they might one day be sitting at a table together, sharing a drink, but Jorge and Mae had hooked up instead.

They were an odd couple, Sally thought, but maybe that was the attraction. Mae was the most fastidious person Sally had ever known. Her office at the college looked like something out of one of the more elegant issues of *Southern Living*. There was a rumor that a speck of dust had lingered in Mae's house for more than an hour, but Sally didn't believe it.

Mae had once confessed to Sally, however, that in spite of her addiction to cleanliness and the Martha Stewart way of life, she was attracted to men who might be both dangerous and sloppy.

Jorge, while Sally had seen no evidence of sloppiness, was certainly on the dangerous side if the rumors about him were to be believed. It was true that he had been in prison. That much had been verified. But the reason for his incarceration was unclear. Some said murder, and that story had never been disproved, though Sally doubted it. One thing was certain: he was an excellent choice to head up the college's program of teaching in the several prison units located near Hughes. Inmates enrolled in college courses could identify with a man who'd been in their place and made a success of his life after his release.

Whatever his past, Jorge had one grievous fault that Sally had recently discovered while talking with Mae. It was a fault that in Sally's mind would have prevented any kind of relationship between them as surely as if Jorge had been an unrepentant serial killer. The sad truth was that he was allergic to cats.

"Of course, I don't have a cat," Mae had told Sally that day in the faculty lounge, without quite implying that cats were filthy, diseased, and most likely covered with fleas. "I know that you do, though, and there's nothing wrong with that. Many lonely people find them to be a comfort."

If it had come down to a decision between Lola and Jorge, Sally wasn't in any doubt about which one she would have chosen, so she wrote off her brief infatuation with Jorge to temporary insanity. And she wrote off Mae's remarks as a result of the same thing.

Sally scooted into the booth across from Vera and Jack, and after they'd ordered their drinks, she asked what they wanted to talk to her about.

Jack looked over his shoulder to see if the server was nearby. She wasn't, but Jack said, "Wait until we have our margaritas."

The drinks arrived served in frosted mugs rimmed with salt. Sally's was frozen, with peach flavoring. Jack and Vera had ordered the "gold" version. Everybody had a taste and nodded with satisfaction.

Along with the drinks, the server had brought a bowl of tortilla chips and two small bowls of salsa, one red, one green. Sally preferred the red, which had little bits of cilantro in it. Sally knew there were people who didn't like cilantro, but she wasn't one of them. She took a chip and dipped out some of the salsa. It wasn't fiery hot, but it would do.

"All right," Sally said when she'd eaten the chip. "Now tell me what all the mystery is."

Jack looked around again. They were seated at the end of the last row of booths, as far from the entrance as they could get.

The closest people were Jorge and Mae, who saw Jack looking in her direction and waved. Jack didn't wave back, but Sally did. She wasn't going to let Mae think she was jealous, because she wasn't.

Jack turned back and looked at Vera, who nodded as if giving him permission, which Sally thought might be exactly the case. Vera wasn't one to let anybody else be in charge.

Jack took a sip of his drink and said, "I had a visit from my friend Weems today. I guess you did, too."

"Yes," Sally said, "and things went downhill after that."

She told them about her little chat with Fieldstone and Roy Don Talon.

"Roy Don should be locked up in one of the prison units at Sugar Land by now," Vera said. "Not serving on the college board."

"They could never prove he had anything to do with the hot car ring," Jack said. "Too bad, if you ask me."

"Did Fieldstone support you against Roy Don?" Vera asked.

"Not exactly," Sally said. "And he's set up a meeting tomorrow with Jennifer Jackson."

"Mothers Against Witchcraft," Vera said.

"That's not all," Jack said. "She and her husband are the leaders of the opposition to the bond issue."

"Fieldstone didn't mention that," Sally said.

"He might not know it."

"He knows a lot about what's going on around town," Sally said. "Especially if it involves the college. That's probably why he agreed to the meeting without asking me. He can't afford to offend any of the opposition and give them something to use against him. I'm sure Fieldstone knew, but I didn't think you were plugged into the community like he is."

Jack didn't say anything in response to that.

"I didn't see any need for a meeting," Sally went on. "I don't know what I can say that I haven't already said. But it makes more sense now."

"The purpose of a witch hunt," Vera told her, "is to make people afraid. Jennifer Jackson is the kind of person who enjoys trying to scare people. Fieldstone should have refused to set up a meeting even if she is opposing the bond issue."

Sally more or less agreed, but she was willing to forgive Fieldstone. She said, "He wasn't as bad as he was earlier in the day

83

when he told me it would be a good idea if I repudiated witchcraft."

"Jack told me about that," Vera said. "I'm glad you told him it was a stupid idea."

Sally had another chip and some more red salsa. Then she had another sip of the peach margarita.

"That's not exactly what I said, but I did tell him that he was being ridiculous. How can I repudiate witchcraft? I can't help it if my husband was distantly related to a woman who was executed for something like that."

"It was the male power structure of the community," Vera said. "They always want women to give in and submit to them. If you've read anything about the witchcraft scare in Salem . . ."

Sally held up a hand. "I read about it every semester for my American literature class. I know more about Cotton Mather and Samuel Sewall than I want to know."

Vera nodded. "Then you know that most of the so-called witches were women who weren't very well liked and had no friends to defend them. They lived outside society's norms. Men have always feared women like that."

"I'm not like that," Sally said. "Am I?"

"Not all of the accused were women," Jack pointed out, hastily changing the subject.

Vera waved him off. "I said *most*. As soon as the governor's wife was accused, what happened?"

"The whole sorry mess came to a screeching halt," Jack said.

"Right. She was a woman with power and powerful friends. Not to mention that her husband was governor. It's always been the powerless who get executed."

Sally had heard that point of view before, as well as just about every other theory about the panic in Salem. It was interesting, but she didn't see where it was leading, and she didn't think of herself as powerless. She was pretty sure Fieldstone didn't, either, and Jennifer Jackson should have known better, too.

"You and Jack didn't bring me here just to talk about the Salem witches and drink margaritas, did you?" she said.

"No," Vera said. "We brought you here for something else."

Sally looked into her glass and saw that her margarita was just about gone. She was feeling a little giddy, too.

"We'd better order some food before you tell me," she said.

"Good idea," Jack said, and looked around for the server, who showed up almost as if she'd popped out of thin air.

Maybe she's a witch, Sally thought. Or maybe I shouldn't have drunk this margarita on an empty stomach.

She ordered a plate of spinach enchiladas, knowing they'd make her feel better. Vera and Jack decided to share chicken fajitas, and when the server was gone, Sally explained that there was no such thing as chicken fajitas. Margaritas always made her a tad garrulous.

Jack and Vera didn't seem interested, and so Sally finished off her drink and had another chip with salsa. She looked across the restaurant and saw Jorge and Mae leaving. Mae smiled and waved again. So did Sally.

The fajitas came sizzling to the table, and Sally's enchiladas arrived at the same time. Sally no longer wanted to talk. She put some salsa on her enchiladas and started eating, while Jack and Vera rolled up chicken, beans, rice, and *pico de gallo* in flour tortillas.

They ate in silence for a while. After she had eaten one entire enchilada, Sally looked up and said, "All right. I feel better now. So tell me what we're doing here."

Vera wiped her mouth with her napkin, while Jack looked around to be sure they weren't being overheard. He was beginning to look to Sally like a snitch in a bad prison movie.

"You know that e-mail about you being a witch?" Vera said.

Sally nodded. "All too well. That's what got me the meetings with Fieldstone. That's why Weems was in my office. As if I were a witch. Did you ever hear of anything so absurd?"

"So you're not a witch?"

"Of course not," Sally said.

Vera looked at her.

"Well," she said. "I am."

9

It was hard to follow up on something like that. Jack fiddled with his fork while Sally just stared at Vera. After a few seconds had passed in silence, Sally looked at Jack.

"Did you know about this?"

Jack nodded. He seemed a little embarrassed.

"It's not like I go around turning people into toads," Vera said.

"You turn me into an animal now and then," Jack said, and Sally had to laugh.

Even Vera smiled. "That's different."

It was getting later, and the restaurant was filling up. Sally said that it might be a good idea for them to finish their meal and then go somewhere else to talk. She didn't think discussing Vera's occult leanings in the Adobe Hacienda was a good idea, no matter how private their booth was.

"We can go to my house," she said. "I'll make some coffee."

"I could use it," Jack said. "That was a strong margarita."

Sally was no longer feeling in the least giddy. She was as sober as she'd ever been. Finding out that a faculty member was a witch had that effect.

Sally arrived at her house first and put the Acura in the garage. She got the Ladysmith out of the trunk and stowed it away before Vera and Jack got there. When the doorbell rang, she'd already started the coffee.

Lola came out of the bedroom to see the visitors. When she'd looked them over with disdain, she went back to the dark room and got under the bed. She wasn't fond of visitors.

Sally ushered her guests back to the kitchen where they sat at the table in the breakfast area.

"The coffee smells good," Jack said. "What kind is it?"

"Hazelnut," Sally told him. "I hope you don't mind flavored coffee."

"It's fine," Jack said, looking at her coffeemaker. "What the heck is that thing?"

"It grinds the beans and then makes the coffee," Sally said. "It tastes fresher that way."

They sat at the table and made small talk about the college until the coffee was ready. Sally got up and poured it into some mugs she'd bought as a gift for a relative. She'd liked them so much that she'd kept them and bought another gift.

When the coffee had cooled a little, Jack took a sip.

"That's really good," he said.

"I'm glad you like it. Now, about this witch business."

"You're thinking about Samantha," Vera said. "Admit it."

"Not to mention Darrin and Endora."

"I always liked Uncle Arthur and Aunt Esmeralda best," Jack said.

"Well," Vera said, "it's not like that at all."

"I had a feeling it wasn't," Sally said. "What *is* it like?"

"First of all," Vera said, "I'm not really a witch. I'm a Wiccan. But it would be hard to explain the difference to somebody like Jennifer Jackson."

"It's not going to be easy to explain it to me, either," Sally said. She took a swallow of coffee and put her mug down on the table. "But you can try."

Vera sighed. She put both hands around her coffee mug as if she were warming them.

"All right. Wicca is a religion. Some

Wiccans think that Wicca and witchcraft are synonyms. Not me. Admittedly, some Wiccans do magic, but I don't. I'm more interested in communing with the Goddess. Witches aren't into that, for the most part. They like doing spells and that sort of thing, mostly they're frauds just doing it to get money from gullible people. But some of them are serious. They're best avoided."

Sally thought about Roy Don Talon. She remembered that the Salem witches had supposedly written their names in the Devil's book.

"So where does Satan come into it?" she asked.

"He doesn't," Vera said. "Not with me or any other Wiccan. Satan is a Christian and Islamic concept. Wiccans don't even recognize his existence. We're pagans, not devil worshipers."

"Pagans, but not devil worshipers?" Sally said. "Forget about explaining things to Jennifer Jackson. I'd like to hear you explain that idea to Roy Don Talon."

"Me, too," Jack said, grinning. "Some people think that anybody who worships in a pagan way is really worshiping Satan. Even if they say they aren't, they're only kidding themselves. Roy Don Talon believes that, I'll bet."

"Are you a Wiccan?" Sally asked him.

"Nope. I'm just dating one. She's goddess enough for me."

Sally thought that Jack's new relationship was making him a little sappy.

"And why is it important that I know about Wiccan business?" she said.

"Because," Vera told her, "you're the one who's being accused of witchcraft. I'm wondering if I'm the real target."

"I don't think so," Sally said. "After all, whoever sent that e-mail was basing it on my last name."

"That could be just a ruse."

Sally didn't think so, and she wondered aloud why anyone would be interested in getting Vera fired.

"Because I'm a Wiccan. You can imagine how that would go over with certain people in this town. Roy Don Talon and Jennifer Jackson aren't the only ones who'd blow their tops if they found out a real witch was teaching their kids."

"I thought you said you weren't a witch."

"I also said it would be hard to explain. Make that *impossible* to explain."

Sally could see her point, but she didn't think Vera had anything to worry about. After all, Vera's name hadn't been in the e-mail. But Sally didn't get a chance to start that discussion again because Vera had something else to say.

"And then there's Harold Curtin's death."

"What does that have to do with you?" Sally asked.

"Nothing, but considering the way he died, people might think that some kind of spell was involved."

"People would be wrong," Sally said. "You can't kill someone with a spell."

"Don't tell a witch that."

Everyone was through with the first cup of coffee, and no one wanted any more. Sally gathered up the cups and set them on the kitchen counter. She turned off the coffeemaker and sat back down at the table.

"Weems thinks Curtin might have been murdered," she said. "But thank goodness he didn't mention any magic spells."

"It's those quotations that keep bothering me," Jack said. "They're both related to witchcraft, and that's why Vera is worried about what people might think. Where did Weems come up with those things? He didn't just grab them out of the air."

Sally had been wondering the same thing. Weems was a dogged investigator and a fairly intelligent man, but he wasn't the kind to come up with two blood-to-drink quotations all by himself.

"He had them written in his little notebook," Jack continued. "I think he copied them down in Harold's apartment. And if he did . . ."

"That would mean someone was trying to cast blame for Curtin's death on a witch," Vera said. "And I'm the only one of those I know. Well, in Hughes. There are plenty of Wiccans in Houston."

"And then there's Seepy Benton," Jack said. "Nobody knows for sure what he is."

Seepy was Dr. C. P. Benton, who preferred to be called by his initials rather than either of his first two names. It hadn't taken long for the initials to elide into the nickname. Benton was the college's director of institutional research. Among other things, he was an adept with computers, could create PowerPoint presentations that captive audiences actually enjoyed, and was a brilliant manipulator of statistics. All those things endeared him to Fieldstone, despite the fact that Seepy was unquestionably a little odd.

A former mathematics instructor, he was enchanted by fractals and chaos theory. He had his own Web site (http://web.wt.net/~

cbenton/welcome.htm), where he explored such things as Jewish mysticism and presented his "song of the week," complete with a video presentation of his own performance of it.

To say that he was a bit different from other administrators at HCC was like saying that a Farrelly brothers movie was a bit different from a Royal Shakespeare Company's performance of *Hamlet*.

"You know, I've wondered about him," Vera said.

Jack laughed. "Join the club."

"I mean I've wondered if he might not be a Wiccan. I know he believes in astrology."

"Only when it's supported by mathematics," Jack said, as if quoting something he'd heard several times.

"Whatever," Vera said. "I still wonder if he's a Wiccan."

"I suppose you have meetings," Sally said.

"Yes. We don't get naked and dance around moonlit graves at midnight, though, if that's what you're thinking."

"I wasn't thinking that."

"I was," Jack said, and Vera punched him on the arm.

"This isn't funny, Jack," she said.

"I wasn't trying to be funny."

"We do believe in the power of the moon, though," Vera said.

"Never mind," Sally said. She wasn't interested in Vera's religious practices at the moment. "You haven't seen Seepy at any of the meetings?"

"Never. But there are several groups besides the one I've joined."

Sally thought that Seepy's possible Wiccan leanings might be worth looking into. The president was counting heavily on Benton's skills in the bond election, and Benton would naturally be antagonistic to Harold Curtin if he was mixed up with the opposition.

"Weems told me that Curtin might have been murdered," Sally said, not that she thought Seepy was a killer. But she also knew you could never be sure about something like that. "And if I know Weems, he doesn't believe in witchcraft or spells. He believes in things he can prove."

"You know," Jack said, "there's a connection between Harold and the Jacksons."

That was interesting, especially given what Sally had just been thinking about Benton.

"You told me that he was involved with

Citizens for Fiscal Responsibility," she said. "What about the Jacksons?"

"I don't know for sure, but I wouldn't be surprised if they were with him on that. For all I know they *are* the Citizens for Fiscal Responsibility."

"Whoever that bunch is, they know a lot about the college," Vera said. "I've seen their ads."

"Curtin was feeding them information," Sally said, sure of it. "He must have been."

Jack shrugged. "I don't know. It's possible."

"You don't seem so sure about it," Sally said, "but you seem to know an awful lot about Harold Curtin and his doings. Is there something you want to tell me, Jack?"

Jack looked around the kitchen. "I think I'd like a little more coffee, after all. You think it's still warm?"

Sally said she was sure it was. She got Jack's cup off the counter and poured coffee in it.

"Vera?" she said.

"No, thanks."

Sally took the coffee to the table and set it in front of Jack. He took a couple of sips.

"We're waiting, Jack," Sally said.

"It's not like Harold and I were friends or anything," Jack said.

"What were you, then?" Vera said.

"I don't know. Maybe he thought we were friends. He used to call me and complain about the college. He said he was going to help defeat the bond issue and then get elected to the board. After that he was going to get rid of Fieldstone."

"Did he really think anyone would vote for him?" Sally asked.

"He seemed to think he had plenty of support."

"Would *you* have voted for him?"

"No, and I never told him that I would. I don't think anybody who worked at the college would vote for him, but that wouldn't have bothered Harold at all. He thought we were all morons."

"Even you?"

"Even me. I told you we weren't friends. But we worked together for a long time, and he probably just needed someone to talk to about his schemes."

"Did he ever mention anyone who might want him dead?" Vera asked.

"That would have been a very long list," Jack said. "Starting with every student who ever took one of his classes. Let's not get too excited here. Maybe Harold died a perfectly natural death."

"Or maybe he didn't," Sally said. She was getting a very bad feeling in the pit of her stomach. Had it been only a few hours ago that she'd thought things were going to be all right? "It's hard to believe that the e-mail and those quotations were just coincidence."

"Sometimes a cigar is just a cigar," Jack said.

Sally sighed. Jack was right. She was getting carried away. Weems's visit had upset her, and even the session on the firing range and the margaritas afterward hadn't completely settled her nerves.

"We aren't getting anywhere with this," she said.

Vera agreed. "Information overload. But it's obvious that something's going on. That e-mail, Curtin's death, that meeting you have with Jennifer Jackson tomorrow, a visit from Weems. It seems to me that they're all connected."

"We don't know that. We should slow down and think things over. Maybe then we can come to some conclusions."

"Come by my office after your meeting tomorrow," Jack told her.

Sally said that she would, and Jack and

Vera left. Sally wondered if they'd go some-where and dance naked under the moon.

"What do you think, Lola?" she said as she walked into the bedroom.

Lola, who was still under the bed, had no comment, so Sally took a shower and went to bed.

The Deposition of Joseph Herrick

The Deposition of Joseph Herrick, Sr., who testifieth and saith that on the first day of March 1692: "I being then Constable for Salem, there was delivered to me by war-rant from the worshipful Jno. Hathorne and Jonathan Corwin, Esqrs. Sarah Good for me to carry to their majesties' gaol at Ipswich, and that night I set a guard to watch her at my own house, namely Samuel Braybrook, Michael Dunell, and Jonathan Baker. And the aforenamed per-sons informed me in the morning that that night Sarah Good was gone for some time from them both bare foot and bare legged. And I was also Informed that that night Elizabeth Hubbard, one of the afflicted persons, complained that Sarah Good came and afflicted her, being bare foot and bare legged."

10

Sally's eight o'clock class on Tuesdays and Thursdays was developmental English, a course designed for students who had somehow managed to graduate from the public schools with few, if any, writing skills.

Some of them had a rudimentary grasp of sentence structure, and could even write a compound sentence on demand. But it was likely to be something like one of her favorites, "Bill have him a coat, but I be cold." It was a compound sentence. There was no way to get around it.

Others had a better command of the proper use of verbs, but they couldn't spell. Sally liked a sentence she'd gotten on one paper in which the student had talked about "bushing his tooths."

Even with all the problems that some students had, however, Sally liked teaching the class. She liked the students, and she liked helping them overcome their more obvious problems.

But today she had trouble keeping her

mind on the students' problems because her sleep had been disturbed by dreams of some ragged woman, Sarah Good most likely, being dragged before a huge wooden structure upon which several men in dark robes sat, looking down on her accusingly and questioning her about things Sally couldn't understand.

In addition, her mind kept drifting to the upcoming meeting with Fieldstone and Jennifer Jackson. She wondered if they would treat her the way the villagers and the judges in Salem had treated Sarah Good.

Sally let the class out a little early, which wouldn't have pleased Dean Naylor had he known about it, and went by her office for a quick chocolate fix before the meeting. She told herself that she'd eat only half a bar, but she wound up eating the whole thing. She told herself that the walk to Fieldstone's office would use up the calories, and if that didn't do it, the meeting would.

When Sally walked into Fieldstone's outer office, Eva Dillon gave her an encouraging smile and picked up the telephone.

"Dr. Good is here to see you," she said. Then, after listening for a couple of seconds, she told Sally that Fieldstone was ready for her. "And the Jacksons are in there, too."

"Both of them?"

Eva nodded. "Both of them."

Sally had understood that only Jennifer would be there, but she didn't suppose that Sherm's presence would make any difference. He was a mousy little man who generally had little to say. Jennifer was the one who did all the talking. The two of them worked together in Sherm's little independent insurance agency, and Sally had heard that they sold quite a few policies. Jennifer was the salesperson. Sherm was the business manager. He sat in the back and spent most of his time in front of a computer.

"You can handle them," Eva said when Sally hesitated outside the door.

"I know," Sally said. "I'm just a little surprised that they're both here."

"If that's a surprise, how about this: Christopher Matthys is in there, too."

"Thanks for the warning," Sally said.

Matthys was the college's attorney, and Sally wasn't really surprised that Fieldstone had asked him to be there. Fieldstone was a careful man, and it was typical of him to have the school's legal representative at a meeting that was likely to be as contentious as the one between Sally and the Jacksons might become. Fieldstone would be hoping that Matthys could prevent Sally from saying something the college would regret.

Sally didn't think he had a chance.

On the other hand, Sally thought, maybe she was doing Fieldstone an injustice. It could be that Matthys was there to defend Sally. She'd have to wait and see.

"If you're not back in a week, can I have your Hershey bars?" Eva asked.

"Bottom drawer, left," Sally said, and opened the door to Fieldstone's office.

Jack Neville had a composition class at eight o'clock on Tuesday mornings. He spent the time discussing an essay that the students had turned in the previous Thursday. He had used his word processor to copy several paragraphs of examples from the papers, then photocopied the examples for distribution to the class. He had also made a transparency of the photocopy so he could use the overhead projector to enlarge the examples on a screen in front of the classroom and point directly to the things he wanted to emphasize.

It was always a challenge to use the overhead in an early class. To do so, Jack had to darken the room, and darkening the room might well lead some students to seize the chance to catch up on some of the sleep they felt they needed. The challenge was in how to make talking about writing errors so exciting that nobody nodded off while he was talking.

It was especially challenging since Jack felt like nodding off himself. Vera hadn't wanted to go home after they left Sally's house, so they had gone to Jack's place. She hadn't left until well after midnight, and because of certain strenuous physical activities they had engaged in, Jack hadn't been able to get right to sleep. Too, his head had been crowded with all kinds of conflicting emotions. As a result, he'd slept only three or four hours, and he was never at his best without sleeping twice that long.

Somehow he managed to get through the class without losing a single student to the sandman. A couple of them had yawned, but then so had Jack, so he couldn't be too critical. As the class ended, he gave them the assignment for Thursday and gathered up his books and papers, which he took back to his office before going off to look for Seepy Benton.

Benton's office wasn't in the administration building, for reasons that weren't exactly clear to Jack. He'd heard that the problem was office space, or lack thereof, in the admin building, but he wasn't sure that was the real reason. He suspected that Fieldstone wouldn't have been comfortable with someone like Benton in an office that was next to his own, or even in the same building.

So Benton was relegated to a space on the second floor of the business building. It was actually a pretty good deal, Jack thought, certainly better than being located right where the president and his minions could keep their eyes on you all the time. Jack would have preferred it that way, and he suspected that Benton did as well.

Jack went into Benton's outer office and asked Molly Evans, the I.R. director's secretary, if Dr. Benton was there. Molly was a smiling woman with a good sense of humor, which was an asset if you were working with Dr. Benton, in whose office there was none of the formality that existed elsewhere on campus. Nobody announced that you were there. Molly just smiled and said, "He's here. Go right in."

Jack went past her and into Seepy's office, which made Sally's look as if it had been cleaned and organized by Mae Wilkins. There were papers everywhere, even stacked in one corner of the room. A guitar case sat on one chair, and hanging on a coatrack were a coonskin cap and a braided leather whip. Some kind of astrological chart covered most of one wall, and on another were framed photographs of fractals. Jack knew that Benton had taken the photographs himself and was rather proud of them, but Jack didn't ask about them because to do so was to risk a lecture on Mandelbrot sets or whatever they were. Jack wasn't sure of the proper term, but he wasn't going to say that either. Benton loved to lecture and would do so at the least opportunity, and Jack wasn't in the mood to talk math.

Benton was sitting at his computer desk, looking at the monitor. While the rest of the office was chaotic, the computer desk was uncluttered. Jack stood and watched as Benton made a few movements with the mouse, clicked to save, and swiveled his chair around.

"What can I do for you, Jack?" Benton asked.

He spoke slowly and reassuringly, perhaps because he had once taught college algebra, a course that Jack knew from his own undergraduate experience could destroy a student's self-esteem faster than a bad complexion or having to drive an inferior car.

In addition to being glacially calm, Benton was a soft-looking teddy bear of a man. Today he wore a Hawaiian shirt with a blue background covered with large white flowers that Jack suspected belonged to no known species growing either on the mainland or the islands. His black beard was shot through with gray, as was the thinning hair that curled wildly on his head.

"Can we talk?" Jack said.

"Sure. Move the guitar and have a seat."

"I meant privately," Jack said, indicating the door that was open to the outer office.

"Molly never listens in. She's afraid I might play something on the guitar and sing along. Which reminds me. I wrote a new song last night. It's called 'Fabric Free.' Would you like to hear it?"

"I wouldn't," Molly called from the other room. "I've already heard it three times."

"Some people have no appreciation for the arts," Benton said, shaking his head as Molly shut the door between the two rooms.

Jack leaned the guitar case against the wall well out of Benton's reach and then sat in the chair.

Benton looked hurt. "I thought an English teacher might appreciate my song. It even rhymes."

"Knowing you," Jack said, "I have a feeling I know what the lyrics of a song called 'Fabric Free' might be about."

"I'm not in my nudist phase anymore." Benton's hurt look became slightly unfocused and faraway. "Those were good times, but Hippie Hollow just isn't the same these days."

Jack was afraid to ask why not, but Benton told him anyway.

"All the people who go there now are as old as I am. Time and gravity can be cruel to the human body, Jack."

Jack said he knew the truth of that all too well.

"So what did you want to talk about, then?" Benton asked. "Did you want me to cast your horoscope? I've been doing a little of that lately to pick up a little extra money. I charge a hundred dollars, but I could give you the faculty discount."

"What's the faculty discount?" Jack asked, suppressing a yawn. He didn't want his horoscope cast, but he was curious.

"You know the faculty discount you get at all the stores in town?"

Jack was puzzled. "I don't get a discount at the stores in town."

"That's right, and I'm giving you the same one."

Jack was never quite sure when Benton was joking, but he assumed that this time he was.

"Thanks," Jack said, "but I'll pass. What I wanted to talk to you about might be a bit related to astrology, though."

"Good. I'm always interested in things like that. What was it, exactly?"

"Harold Curtin," Jack said.

11

"Come in, Dr. Good," Fieldstone said as she entered his office. Matthys stood up and greeted her, smiling as if to reassure her that he was indeed on her side. Fieldstone stood as well, but only to offer Sally a seat. He and Matthys were dressed in navy-blue suits that were all but identical.

The Jacksons stayed right where they were, hardly bothering to spare Sally a glance. They sat in their chairs, backs straight, eyes forward, knees together.

When Sally had taken a seat beside Matthys on the leather couch, Fieldstone went back behind his desk. The Jacksons were facing the desk, in profile to the couch.

Fieldstone didn't lighten the atmosphere a bit when he said that the meeting was being recorded. He'd gotten permission from the Jacksons before Sally arrived. After that little announcement, he performed all the unnecessary introductions and then said, "I think Mrs. Jackson would like to speak first."

"Yes, I would," she said.

She was painfully thin, Sally thought, almost anorexic. Her fingers were long, just skin and bone. Her hair looked great, though. It was cut quite short and almost made her angular face look pretty. If she and Sally had been friends, Sally would have asked where she got her hair done.

Sherm Jackson just looked average. He was the kind of man who could disappear in a crowd of three. He wore a gray jacket, gray pants, and a nondescript tie. Sally wondered if he would speak at all during the meeting.

Jennifer Jackson turned slightly in her chair. Not much. Not enough so that she would have to meet Sally's eye, but enough so that she would seem to be talking to both Sally and Fieldstone.

"Yesterday I got a very troubling e-mail," she said. "It was about Dr. Good. Here's a copy of it."

She handed a piece of paper to Fieldstone, who hardly looked at it.

"For the record," Fieldstone said, "I got the same e-mail. It says that Dr. Sally Good, a member of the HCC faculty, is a witch, descended from Sarah Good, notorious witch of the seventeenth century, executed for the crime of witchcraft in 1692.

A ridiculous charge, as Dr. Good will explain. The campus police are working with one of our computer specialists to see if they can find out where the e-mail originated."

"It had a return address."

"Which is a fake," Fieldstone said. "We're working on it, however, and we'll find out the real sender."

"It doesn't really matter," Jennifer said, turning a bit more toward Sally. "I don't think the college needs an instructor whose past is so questionable. You might remember that she's defended witchcraft before."

"That's not true," Sally said.

"I haven't finished," Jennifer said. "Dr. Fieldstone said I could have my say, without interruption."

Fieldstone hadn't mentioned that little fact to Sally, who gave him a reproachful look. Fieldstone made no response except to say, "Please go on, Mrs. Jackson."

Sally started to object, but Matthys nudged her elbow. He was still smiling, so Sally settled back on the couch.

"Well," Jennifer said, "when an organization of which I'm a member tried to cleanse the local library of several books about witches, Dr. Good stepped right up to stop us. Everyone knows those books are just thinly disguised satanic tracts that glorify witchcraft. Who knows how many children have been lured into witchcraft by reading them?"

"I do," Sally said. "None. And while we're at it, please tell me how many times Satan is mentioned in those books. Have you ever read them?"

Jennifer was shocked. "Of course I haven't. Why would I do something like that?"

"To find out if what you're talking about is true or just a pile of . . . rubbish. I've read the books, every one of them. Satan is never mentioned at all."

Jennifer's hands clenched. "Dr. Fieldstone said I could finish without being interrupted."

"I forgot," Sally lied.

Matthys muffled a derisive snort, but Sally heard it. She ignored him. Jennifer either didn't hear or didn't care.

"As I was saying, Dr. Good has defended witchcraft before. Now we find out that she's a descendant of a witch who was hanged for her satanic practices. I don't think we need her teaching students from our community."

"That's enough," Sally said, standing. "I

don't care what Dr. Fieldstone told you. I'm not going to sit here and listen to that kind of slander without having something to say about it. It is slander, isn't it, Mr. Matthys."

Matthys stood beside her. "It certainly sounds like it. She's implying that you're unfit for your profession, and if that's untrue, it just might be actionable."

"And we have it on tape," Sally said.

"But I'm just repeating what I received on my computer!"

"Repeating a libel would still be slander," Matthys said. "We'll take action against the sender of the e-mail as soon as we find out who that is."

Jennifer looked pained. "But it's true that Dr. Good defended witchcraft. If it hadn't been for her and a few of her friends, those books wouldn't be in the library now."

"I was defending the freedom to read, not witchcraft," Sally said, resisting the urge to add, "You idiot." Name-calling would get her nowhere. "And as Dr. Fieldstone told you, my late husband was a distant relative of Sarah Good, not me."

"I think there's a lot more to the story than that," Jennifer said.

"And what's that?"

"I think you put a curse on Harold Curtin and killed him."

"Harold Curtin?" Seepy Benton said. "What about him?"

"He's dead."

"I know that, but I don't see what it has to do with me."

"You're heading up the college's campaign to get the bond issue passed. Harold was one of the opposition leaders."

"I know that, too. What's your point?"

Jack explained what Sally had told him about Weems's suspicions.

"So you think I killed Harold so we could win the election?"

"No," Jack said. "But Weems is acting suspicious of Sally, and even of me."

"You've been in trouble with him before."

"That wasn't my fault," Jack said. "Anyway, what I'd like to know is who might want to get rid of Harold."

"Except for all his former students, most of the faculty he knew, and nine-tenths of the people he met, I have no idea."

"You know something about this bond election. You know who's for it and against it. You might know if Harold had made any new enemies."

"Have you heard about the Citizens for Fiscal Responsibility?"

Jack said he had.

"And did you know that Harold was involved with them?"

Jack admitted that he'd heard it from a pretty good source, Curtin himself.

"Other people are in the group, but Harold was helping them quite a bit. He was giving them information about college operations and finances, but he was exaggerating. They've used some of the exaggerations in their advertisements."

"Like the one that says taxes will go up by thirty percent if the bond passes?"

"No. And anyway, that's not an exaggeration."

"It's not?" Jack didn't like paying taxes any more than anybody else, even though he knew his money was going to support the college. "No wonder there's opposition."

Benton settled back in his chair, laced his fingers together, and rested his hands on his stomach. Jack knew that he was about to get a lecture. He hoped it would be a short one.

"There are ways to use facts to make them appear much worse than they are," Benton said. "While it's true that there would be a thirty percent tax increase if the bond passes, what's left unsaid is that because college taxes are so low, the increase would amount to about seventy-five dollars a year for the average taxpayer. That would be six dollars and twenty-five cents a month. I think everyone could afford that."

Jack thought the Citizens for Fiscal Responsibility were dirty fighters to twist things and make them appear much worse than they actually were, but dirty tactics were to be expected in any kind of campaign.

"If that's not one of the exaggerations you were talking about," he said, "what is?"

"The business about administrative travel," Benton said. "Did you see that ad in the newspaper about the college board's trip to Hawaii?"

Jack remembered that one. There was a photo of the board members that had been altered to show them all dressed in grass skirts. The caption had been something like *Board members party in the islands while you suffer in the Texas heat.*

"That trip wasn't paid for by the college," Benton said. "Even though it was legitimate college business. The Hawaii meeting was an important training session, and it was attended by college board members from all over the country."

Jack didn't question the meeting's importance, though it did seem to him that while college boards and presidents held their meetings in places like Hawaii, San Francisco, and Key West, meetings for college faculty were more likely to be in Dallas, Houston, or Austin.

"Who paid for the trip?" Jack asked.

"The board members paid for it themselves, out of their own pockets. The ad sticks to the truth, but like the one about the thirty percent increase, it leaves something unsaid. You might have noticed that it didn't say the college paid for the trip. It just implied it."

Jack couldn't remember the ad exactly, but he was sure Benton was right.

"Are you telling me that one of the board members might have killed Curtin because of that ad?"

"No. I'm telling you that none of them liked him very much. But as we know, that would put them on a very long list."

Jack didn't blame the board members for not liking Curtin. And thinking about his past experiences, he believed that at least one board member, Roy Don Talon, was capable of murder.

"And don't forget Larry Lawrence," Benton said.

Larry was easy to forget, Jack thought. He'd been Fieldstone's administrative assistant for years, longer than Jack had been at the college, until he'd taken early retirement a couple of years previously. He'd been the perfect man to play second fiddle. He was quiet, unobtrusive, glad to work behind the scenes and let the Big Guy get all the credit.

"Why would Larry be a suspect?" Jack asked.

"I didn't say he was a suspect. He might be, but he wasn't against Harold's stand on the bond issue. He was helping him."

Jack said he didn't believe it. "Larry was always a strong supporter of the college."

"That's right. He was. You English teachers always use the right verb. He's not anymore."

"Why not?"

"We administrators have to keep some secrets. Otherwise we wouldn't be any better than the faculty members."

"If the cops come and ask you, you'll tell them. Surely you like me better than you like the cops."

Benton looked over to where his guitar case leaned against the wall.

120

"Maybe the cops would listen to my new song."

"No, they wouldn't. They'd haul you in and give you the third degree. Believe me, I know."

"Maybe you do, at that. All right. This has to do with cops. You know how Chief Desmond has a thing for younger women?"

Jack knew. There were few if any real secrets at the college. But sometimes things could be successfully covered up if the right people worked on doing it. Desmond was one of the right people.

"He hasn't been dating students, has he?" Jack said.

While Fieldstone felt that the personal lives of college employees were their own business, there was a college rule against fraternizing with students. Faculty members had been known to violate the rule in the past, and it had gotten them into trouble.

"Desmond's not crazy," Benton said. "He's just having a late midlife crisis."

"He's been having it for about fifteen years."

"Possibly. Anyhow, one of the younger women he liked was Larry's daughter."

"You said *liked*."

"There's that verb tense thing again. And you're right. I did use the past tense. Desmond dumped her, and she went through a bad time. She was teaching in Houston, but she quit her job, moved back home with the Lawrences, and developed an unfortunate substance abuse problem."

"How unfortunate?" Jack asked.

"Bad enough. She's doing better now, but Larry blames the college for the whole thing. We're not liable in any way, of course. What employees do on their own time isn't any of our business, as long as it doesn't affect their ability to do their jobs."

And as long as they stayed away from students, Jack thought. And knowing how litigious people were these days, Jack was surprised Larry hadn't sued the school. However, if Larry had joined the anti-bond issue crowd, he had found another way to get his revenge.

"Their real reason for opposing the bond issue isn't that they don't like taxes," Benton said. "It's not even that they don't like the college."

"It's not?" Jack said. "Then what is it?"

"They blame Fieldstone for all their troubles," Benton said.

"Harold blamed Dr. Good, too."

"Most of their troubles then. At any rate,

Larry and Harold want to get Fieldstone fired. Or to get the verbs right, Larry *does* and Harold *did*."

"I knew Harold did. He was going to run for the board. I didn't know about Larry."

Benton spread his arms. "Now you know all my secrets. I'll be booted out of the Administrators' Guild."

"Do you think Fieldstone would kill anyone?"

"He's a college president, isn't he?" Benton said. "What do you think?"

12

Sally sat in her office behind her locked door while she ate a Hershey bar and seethed. She seldom felt a need for privacy while at work, but this time the circumstances called for extraordinary measures.

She could understand why Fieldstone had arranged the meeting she had just left, but that didn't make her feel any better about it. Jennifer Jackson hadn't been content to accuse her of being a witch. She'd had to accuse her of murder, too.

Of course, Matthys had told Sally that Jennifer had done no such thing. She'd *alleged* it, but she hadn't made a direct accusation. So there was no slander involved.

For a few seconds there in Fieldstone's office, Sally had wished that she really were a witch, one of those who knew how to cast transformation spells. If that had been the case, Jennifer would have been changed in the blink of an eye into some kind of disgusting bug and left to squirm on Fieldstone's rug until someone stepped on her, or called the exterminator.

But, as Sally wasn't a witch, Jennifer had left the office with her husband, who hadn't opened his mouth the entire time except to breathe, looking smug and satisfied as if she'd achieved some kind of victory.

Fieldstone had assured Sally that wasn't true. He didn't believe in witches, though he still thought it would be a good idea for Sally to make some kind of public statement that she didn't either.

It wasn't as bad as asking her to repudiate witchcraft, she supposed, but she didn't intend to make any public statements. After all, she happened to know a witch, or a Wiccan, which was more or less the same thing in her opinion, no matter what Vera had said about the difference.

When she'd told Fieldstone that she was acquainted with a witch, he looked as if he'd been hit between the eyes with a sledgehammer.

"You're joking," he'd managed to say after he recovered.

"Not a bit. It's not something I'd joke about."

Fieldstone opened and closed his mouth like a goldfish looking out of a small bowl.

Matthys seemed to think the whole scene was funny. It was nice to know there was a lawyer with a sense of humor, but Sally didn't think there was anything amusing about the situation.

And there wasn't anything amusing about the fact that she'd already eaten two Hershey bars in one day. She was going to balloon up another dress size if she didn't watch out, and it would all be Jennifer Jackson's fault.

Yet another thing that steamed Sally, and a more serious one, was the way the Jacksons and even Fieldstone were condemning witches in general and Sarah Good in particular, as if the foolishness of 1692 hadn't been exposed again and again in the more than three hundred years since the witchcraft trials.

Sally was saved from her own blood pressure when someone knocked on the door. She couldn't continue brooding in a locked office, as everyone knew she rarely closed the door. Sooner or later she was going to have to come out.

She popped the last bite of candy into her mouth, wadded up the candy bar wrapper, and threw it in the trash can. She wiped her fingers on a tissue that she pulled from the box she kept on her desk for the convenience of students who started crying while explaining their troubles to her. The troubles usually came down to the fact that the students' instructors hated them with the result that they were making Cs instead of As. Or possibly some cruelly unjust instructor wouldn't allow makeup work to some poor student who had missed two weeks of class to go on family vacation that couldn't be taken any time except in the middle of the college semester.

Sally checked her fingers to be sure there were no telltale chocolate stains remaining. There weren't, so the tissue followed the candy wrapper, and Sally got up to open the door.

Standing there waiting for her was Samuel Winston. He looked at her with the big round eyes that had caused his students to nickname him "the Owl." Sally had the impression that he thought teaching in a community college was beneath a man of his powerful intellect, and sometimes his students got the same idea.

"Yes, Samuel?" Sally said. He was the kind of person who insisted on being called by his full name. No shortening to *Sam* was allowed.

Winston blinked twice. Then he said,

"Someone stole my stapler. I left it in the copy room for a few minutes, and when I came back it was gone."

Ah, Sally thought. Things are getting back to normal.

Finding the stapler didn't require the deductive powers of Sherlock Holmes. The copier room was located right down the hall from Sally's office, and Wynona Reed could see the entrance from her desk. Hardly a person who entered the copy room escaped her constant vigilance.

Sally told Winston to follow her, and they went over to Wynona's desk.

"Tell her," Sally said.

Winston blinked.

"It was Baldree," Wynona said before Samuel could get a word out. "Big black stapler, right? I saw her leave the copy room with it. She wasn't carrying it when she went in there."

Sally thanked her and told Samuel to come along. He trotted along behind her as she led him to Ellen Baldree's office. Ellen, who thought she should have been named department chair when Sally was hired, had never liked Sally, but she hadn't been openly defiant. She had adopted the "I can last longer than you" attitude and settled in to wait for Sally's firing. As it hadn't happened yet, Ellen had become increasingly sullen around Sally, sometimes even openly resentful, but she was still a professional in the classroom. She had even volunteered to take some computer classes so she could teach the department's WebCT classes, and she had developed into quite a computer whiz.

The door to Ellen's office was open. The office was so small that Ellen's desk and bookshelves barely left room for her office chair. Sally and Winston had to stand outside the door to talk to her.

"I think you took Samuel's stapler from the copy room by mistake."

Ellen shook her head, and Sally noticed, not for the first time, how very black Ellen's hair was. As Ellen was around fifty-five, Sally was sure the color wasn't natural, and it didn't make Ellen look any younger.

"That's it," Winston said, pointing through the doorway to a stapler that sat on Ellen's desk atop a stack of photocopied student essays. "My name and office number are scratched into the metal on the side."

Sally stepped as far into the crowded office as she could and tipped the stapler over. She saw S. *Winston A-175* on the metal.

"I guess I made a mistake," Ellen said. "I thought I took my own stapler with me. It must be around here somewhere."

Sally picked up the stapler and handed it to Winston, who thanked her and went away.

"I hope you don't think I took it on purpose," Ellen said when he was gone.

Although Sally did think exactly that, she didn't want to destroy anyone's hopes. So she said, "If you need a new stapler, you can get one at the bookstore and charge it to the departmental budget."

"Someone stole my stapler. It looked just like that one, and I thought I'd found mine." Sally didn't mention the name scratched on the stapler's side, and Ellen continued. "You always make such a big deal about what a small budget we have and how we should all try to avoid spending money that I try not to charge things at the bookstore. I'll buy my own stapler."

Staplers disappeared now and then, Sally knew. People left them in classrooms, and when they went back to get them, the staplers were gone. Students, and even instructors, seemed to think that anything sitting unclaimed in plain sight was there for the taking.

"You don't have to buy your own stapler. I think the college can afford to pay for one. I might even have a spare in the office. I'll go have a look."

"Don't go to any trouble on my account," Ellen said.

"It's no trouble at all," Sally said.

She went back to her office and looked around in all the desk drawers. Sure enough, there was an old black stapler down in the back of one of them. She filled it with staples and tried it out. It worked just fine, so she took it back around to Ellen's office.

"It's a little rusty underneath," Sally said. "But it seems to be working."

"Thanks," Ellen said, but her tone wasn't grateful.

"You're welcome," Sally said, and left it at that.

She returned to her office and looked around for her world literature textbook since she had to teach a class at eleven o'clock, which was only minutes away. She was always punctual in meeting her classes in the hope that her own dependability would encourage her students to be equally reliable. The hope was seldom borne out, but Sally kept trying.

She located the text under a stack of papers and fished it out. She got her grade book out of the desk drawer and started out the door.

Vera Vaughn nearly bumped into her. Sally jumped back, startled.

"I'm sorry," Vera said. "I wanted to catch you before you went to class. We have to talk."

"About what?"

"Harold Curtin. He was a witch."

From Cotton Mather's
The Wonders of the Invisible World

Now, by these confessions [of those condemned in Salem] 'tis agreed that the Devil has made a dreadful knot of witches in the country, and by the help of witches has dreadfully increased that knot: that these witches have driven a trade of commissioning their confederate spirits to do all sorts of mischiefs to the neighbors, whereupon there have ensued such mischievous consequences upon the bodies and estates of the neighborhood, as could not otherwise be accounted for. . . ."

13

Sally couldn't quite believe what she'd just heard.

"What? Harold? A witch?"

"We can't talk here," Vera said. "Where are you going for lunch?"

Sally never went anywhere for lunch. She usually brought something from home, a sandwich or some fruit, and ate in her office.

"I'm staying here," she said.

"That won't do. I don't want to talk about this here. I'll come by for you after class. Don't dawdle."

Vera nodded and left. Sally went on to her class, but she could hardly keep her mind on the assignment, which was Euripides' *Medea*.

It seemed to Sally that she was encountering witches at every turn. Medea herself had been a witch, and a vengeful woman besides. Her husband, Jason, who had quite an ego, had decided to take himself another wife, and that turned out to be a big mistake. He'd been sure that his wife would see nothing wrong with his plan and that she would understand why he was leaving her. She didn't. A witch like Medea would be a formidable enemy, Sally thought.

For the benefit of the class, at least those who were listening, Sally went into the play's backstory before she began discussing the work itself. She knew that a hundred years ago, maybe even sixty or seventy years ago, college students would have had a solid background knowledge of Greek heroes like Jason and that the story of his quest for the Golden Fleece, and how he had obtained it with Medea's help, would be familiar to them. You couldn't count on anything like that today, however.

Although she tried to be thorough, Sally was sure there were things she was leaving out or glossing over. Her mind kept wandering as she thought of Jennifer Jackson's smugness and of Harold Curtin's death. And of the news that Harold had been a witch.

Harold and Medea. Now that would have been a pair, Sally thought.

And Medea and Sarah Good. Certainly the ancient Greek witch could have taught the hapless Sarah something about the power of witchcraft, though Sarah's final curse seemed to have been pretty effective.

Somehow Sally muddled through the class and escaped before any of the students could trap her at the desk and ask questions. As a rule, she was glad to stay after class and talk, but today was different. She couldn't dawdle. Vera had given her an order.

When Sally got back to her office, Vera was waiting.

"My car's in the parking lot, and Jack's already there," she said.

Vera was dressed in black jeans, a black shirt, and black boots. She wore a black scarf around her neck. All she needed was a whip. Not many women could carry off that look, Sally thought, but Vera could.

Sally put her textbook on the desk and put her grade book in the drawer where she kept it. Then she followed Vera out of the building.

It was another swampy day, and Sally could feel her clothes wilting against her before they got to the Navigator, where Jack was sitting in the passenger seat. The windows were down, but that was only so Jack didn't suffocate. Having them open wouldn't make him any cooler.

Vera, appropriately enough, Sally thought,

got into the driver's seat, while Sally climbed into the back. She didn't want to dwell on the symbolism of that. As soon as the doors shut, Vera started the engine and turned the air conditioner on high.

"Where are we going?" Sally asked as the cooling breeze from the vents poured over her.

"The Tea Room," Vera said. "It was Jack's choice."

The unimaginatively named Tea Room was the newest restaurant in Hughes. Sally had never been there, but she had heard about it. The menu consisted mostly of different kinds of flavored tea and coffee, along with soup and sandwiches that Sally suspected didn't have any crusts on them.

"Have you been there?" she asked Jack, who didn't seem like the tearoom type.

Jack half-turned in the seat so he could see Sally. "I was there the other day. The owner is Rick Centner. You may remember him. He was a student at the college about ten years ago."

Sally hadn't been at HCC for ten years. And she still wondered why Jack was visiting a tearoom.

"I went to one of the poetry readings," he said. "You must know about those."

Sally knew. She'd gotten an invitation in

the mail, and she'd seen the ads in the Hughes newspaper.

"I was afraid it would be too painful," she said, thinking about some of the poems that had been submitted for the Hughes literary magazine.

"Some of our creative writing students were there. It wasn't as bad as I thought it might be. Rick's also hung some paintings from our art department. He's doing what he can to give the place a little class and get some customers at the same time."

Sally figured he'd get some of the friends of the poetry readers, along with the friends and families of the art students. She supposed it was a good start. She couldn't think who else in Hughes would go somewhere to hear poetry or to look at paintings and watercolors.

"How was the food?"

"There wasn't much of it," Jack said, which more or less confirmed Sally's suspicions, but she didn't care. She hadn't planned to eat much, anyway.

The Tea Room was located near Hughes's small downtown area. It was in an old house that had been remodeled and furnished with tables and chairs. The side yard had been graveled over to make the parking lot, which was shaded by oak trees that had been there long before the house was built and even before the town had been established. Their limbs spread out over the entire parking lot, shading it almost completely.

"Rick needs to have the trees thinned," Jack said as they got out of the Navigator. "If a bad storm comes through here, it'll tear those trees to pieces."

Sally hoped that didn't happen. The oak trees that grew all over town were the best thing about Hughes. She wouldn't want to lose a one of them.

They entered the Tea Room through what had been the front door of the old house, and as soon as they were inside, Sally noticed two things, the paintings on the walls and a Buddy Holly song that was playing on the sound system, "Rave On." She gave Jack an accusing look.

"Now I understand why you chose this place."

Jack grinned. "I can't help it if Rick has good taste in music."

Rick himself came into the foyer to greet them. He had brown hair and a welcoming smile.

"Hi, Mr. Neville," he said. "And Miss Vaughn. I had you for sociology about ten years ago."

Vera nodded and introduced Sally.

"I'm glad to see some more of the college faculty," Rick said. "I need all the help I can get to get established."

"We'll do what we can," Jack said. "Could you seat us in the pantry?"

"As a matter of fact, I can."

Rick took three menus from a holder on the door frame and led them through a couple of rooms that, if not crowded, at least had several people in them. Sally saw one of the young waiters glance her way, and she thought she recognized him. He was probably a former student of hers, but he turned away and went into the kitchen too quickly for her to be sure.

Rick led them to a very small room that was located behind what Sally thought must have been the kitchen. It would have made a nice-sized walk-in pantry, though it now held one small table and four chairs. The table was covered by a real tablecloth. The napkins were real cloth, too. There were no paintings on the wall. Instead there were framed black-and-white photographs of Buddy Holly and a couple of other people that Sally didn't recognize.

Rick pulled out Sally's chair for her, but Sally noticed that he didn't do the same for Vera. He must have remembered her fairly well.

"I'll send someone to take your order in a minute," Rick said when they were seated.

Jack thanked him, and Sally opened her menu to the sound of Buddy Holly singing "Not Fade Away." The items on the menu were what Sally had expected. People who liked chicken salad could have it on a croissant, on wheat bread, or on white. She decided to go for the wheat. There was a "soup of the day," too, but Sally didn't want soup.

She asked Jack about the photographs, and he told her that they were of the Big Bopper and Ritchie Valens, the other two singers who had died on the plane carrying Buddy Holly. Sally thought that was a little morbid for a tearoom, but Jack thought it was a touching tribute to the day the music died.

"That's a line from 'American Pie,'" Jack said.

Sally said she knew that. "And it's as morbid as the pictures."

"Maybe," Jack said. "One thing's for sure, though. It's not true. The music never really died. We're listening to it right now."

And they were. Buddy Holly sang about

Peggy Sue exactly the way he had forty years previously.

Sally couldn't decide if that was morbid or not. She was saved from commenting when a young woman arrived to take their order. Her name was Madison, and she was a student in Sally's composition class.

"Hi, Madison," Sally said. "I'd like chicken salad on whole wheat. And plain unsweetened iced tea."

Madison managed not to gape the way some students did when they saw their instructors outside the classroom. Sometimes it appeared to amaze them that teachers ate, bought groceries, or went to the movies like actual human beings.

After Madison had left, Sally said, "Now, Vera, just how did you find out that Harold Curtin was a witch?"

"She used her supernatural powers," Jack said, then winced as if someone had kicked him under the table. Sally was pretty sure that someone had.

"I didn't use anything more supernatural than the telephone," Vera said. "This morning I got a call from a friend in Houston. Her beliefs are pretty standard for a Wiccan, but she happens to know a few people who don't believe in the three-fold law."

"I don't even know what that is," Sally said. She was finding it a little difficult to keep up with all the new things she was learning about witchcraft.

" 'All the good that a person does to another returns threefold in this life; harm is also returned threefold,' " Vera said. "That's what Wiccans believe. But some witches who follow another path don't believe it in the least. They believe in doing harm. My friend knows some people like that."

"Some people can twist anything good and make it bad," Jack said.

Sally couldn't tell whether he was serious. Vera didn't kick him under the table this time, so maybe he was. Or maybe Vera just thought he was.

The tea came, and Sally tried it. It wasn't sweetened, so she was satisfied.

"You mentioned something yesterday about people who cast spells for money," Sally said to Vera.

"Those aren't the ones I'm talking about. Those are just charlatans for the most part, and they do love charms and ridiculous things like that. I'm talking about the ones that should be avoided."

"So why is your friend mixed up with them?"

"She's not. Or not really. You know how gossip gets around on the grapevine at the college?"

Sally nodded. In her experience, there was no better example of the grapevine at work than an institution for postsecondary education. People like Troy Beauchamp made everyone's business their business. Spreading the word was like a religion to them, and they were everywhere in the academic world.

"There are grapevines everywhere," Vera said. "Even in the world of Wicca. So my friend heard something from a friend who'd heard it from another friend. You know how it is."

Sally knew how it was, all right, and she knew that the result was sometimes a distorted version of the truth. The distortions, like the thunderstorms that frequently roamed the Gulf Coast area, varied in size and intensity, but they were always present. Sally was about to mention that fact when Madison appeared with their food.

Jack had gone for the soup, which was cheese with broccoli, along with honey ham on a croissant. Vera had ordered the chicken salad on whole wheat as Sally had done. The sandwiches didn't have crusts. Sally took a bite of her sandwich. It was quite good, and she began eating to the accompaniment of Buddy Holly singing about an unusual weather condition: it was raining in his heart.

After she'd eaten a couple of bites of the sandwich, Sally asked Vera how she knew the information she'd received was reliable.

"I don't know that it is," Vera said, "but it's interesting whether it's reliable or not."

"Then why don't you tell us what it is," Jack said.

"I told you. Harold was a witch. He joined a coven in Houston about a month ago."

"Why would he do a thing like that?" Sally said.

"I don't know, but it makes his death seem even more suspicious, don't you think? He could even have been killed by someone in his coven if he was suspected of being a spy or of revealing their secrets."

"I don't see how all this information we're getting fits together," Sally said.

Jack said he didn't see it, either, but that there was a common theme.

"It all has to do with witchcraft. Think about those notes Weems read to us. And then there's the e-mail that went out about you. There's something funny going on, but I can't figure out what it is."

He went on to tell them about his visit with Seepy Benton and what he'd learned.

"He does horoscopes for money?" Sally said. "Isn't there some college policy about that?"

"Nope," Jack said. "Plenty of people at the college have second jobs. Seepy's is just a little more unusual than most of them. It's the bit about Desmond that's interesting."

"I knew about that," Sally said. "Troy told me."

"You didn't tell me," Jack said, looking hurt.

"I try not to pass things like that along. They just hurt innocent people. Besides, I didn't know the part about the Lawrence woman's substance abuse problem. What does that have to do with Curtin, anyhow?"

Jack explained that Larry had turned against the college and was working with Harold and the Citizens for Fiscal Responsibility. Sally hadn't known about that, so obviously Troy didn't, either. He'd have been in her office in a shot with information like that if he'd had it.

"You don't think Larry killed Harold, do you?" Sally said. "I mean, he might want Desmond out of the way, but not Harold."

"I don't know that there's any connection. I'm just telling you what I found out. We have to get all the information we can if we're going to solve the crime."

"Hold on a minute there, bub," Vera said. "We're not going to solve any crime. This isn't a meeting of the HCC branch of Scotland Yard. Or even of the HCC branch of the Nancy Drew fan club. The only thing I care about is helping Sally and setting the record straight about witches. Without having my name mentioned, of course. The police can solve the crime. That's what they're paid to do."

"Yeah," Jack said, "but sometimes they arrest the wrong people."

"I know," Vera said. "Including you. But they let you go, and it's not a good idea to get involved with them unless we have to. I think the best thing for us to do is keep our heads down and stay out of the way."

"Weems isn't going to let us keep our heads down," Jack said. "He's already been by to see me and Sally. He thinks we're involved."

"Grasping at straws," Vera said. "That's all he's doing. And remember, we don't even know that Harold was murdered."

"If he was, the police hadn't told anyone by this morning," Sally said. "I listened to

146

the news on the way to school, and there was nothing like that mentioned."

"My friend hadn't heard even that much," Vera said. "But someone had heard something. Otherwise the story about Harold's connection with witchcraft wouldn't have been making the rounds."

Jack ate the last bite of his sandwich and wiped a crumb off his chin.

"I still think we're in trouble," he said.

"Not yet," Vera said. "I say we teach our classes and leave the investigation to the professionals."

"All right," Jack said. "But I'm predicting trouble."

"You're such a pessimist."

"You just wait and see who's right," Jack said. "I'll bet it's me."

"*I*," Vera said. "You're an English teacher, after all. You of all people should try to have some standards."

"When I'm speaking informally, I can say *me*. That's acceptable. Tell her, Sally."

Sally didn't want to be the mediator, and she didn't want to explain levels of usage. She didn't want to be a crime fighter, either.

"Write a letter to 'Ask Mr. Grammar Person,'" she said.

14

Contrary to Jack's prediction, Sally didn't have any trouble for the first part of that afternoon, unless grading papers could be considered trouble. She supposed that it could in some cases.

A little later, things took a turn for the worse. A. B. D. Johnson dropped by her office to complain that someone had moved the overhead projector from the room where he taught composition.

"I don't see how they expect us to teach if they don't provide the right equipment," he said.

This was a mild complaint, coming from A.B.D. The initials before his name hadn't been given to him at birth. He had earned them by virtue of having left graduate school after completing his course work for the doctorate but never having written his dissertation. A.B.D. meant *all but dissertation,* though nobody ever called him that to his face. Perhaps because of his frustration at not having received a degree that would have qualified him for a bigger paycheck, he spent a lot of his time complaining about things at the college. Sally didn't bother to ask him who "they" were, for in A.B.D.'s life "they" were the vast forces forever arrayed against him.

Or maybe, Sally thought, the forces arrayed against A.B.D. were only half-vast.

"The state's having serious budget problems," she said. "And you should know by now that the first cuts the legislature makes are always in education. We're talking about a state where more than a hundred and eighty million dollars was cut from the high school textbook budget. Some students are using books fourteen or fifteen years old. And the TIF funding has been scrapped besides. That's a huge loss of money for public schools and libraries."

A.B.D. plainly wasn't concerned about high school students who were using textbooks that were old and out of date because the legislature didn't provide money for new ones, or whether libraries could buy new computer equipment. He was concerned about his own situation.

"I read about those budget cuts," he said, "but how much can an overhead cost? I can't do my job without one. If I can't have one of my own, I want you to find out who's taking the one I've been using and moving it out of the classroom. And I want you to make sure it doesn't disappear again."

Sally told him that she'd do what she could, but she didn't make any promises. She didn't think it would be as easy to find out who'd moved the overhead as it had been to find out who'd taken Samuel Winston's stapler.

After A.B.D. left, Sally graded a few more papers, wondering when the phrase *a lot* had become one word in the minds of so many students. It had been years since she'd first noticed it, so long that she couldn't remember. She had decided to grade one more paper and leave for home, but the ringing of the telephone interrupted her. It was Eva Dillon, who said that Fieldstone wanted to see Sally right away.

"He has Chief Desmond with him," Eva said, "and Frankie Gomez is there, too."

Frankie was the head of the computer center, so Sally thought maybe something had been discovered about the malicious e-mail. She left the office in such a hurry that she didn't even finish grading the paper she'd already started.

"They all looked very serious," Eva said when Sally walked into the office. "I hope everything's all right."

"I'm sure it is," Sally told her. "I think it's about that e-mail."

She didn't have to explain which e-mail she meant. Eva, like everyone else, had received a copy of it.

"Go on in and find out," Eva said, and Sally did.

Eva had been right, Sally discovered. Everyone in Fieldstone's office looked as serious as if there had just been some terrible catastrophe, like the school's funding being cut yet again. Even Frankie Gomez, normally the sunniest of people, looked grim. She had lustrous black hair that Sally envied, and eyes that were equally black. She was attractive even when she looked grim.

Sally took her usual seat on the couch. Frankie, whose actual name was Francisca, was beside her, and Desmond was in one of the chairs. For a second or two nobody said anything. Sally would have tried to lighten the mood, but she didn't think it was her place, and she didn't want to seem foolish if there was really something serious going on.

Desmond moved around in the chair like a man with a serious wedgie. Sally hoped he was as uncomfortable as he looked. She wasn't too fond of him in the first place, and what she'd learned from Jack about Larry Lawrence's daughter's problems hadn't helped. Desmond looked at Fieldstone, who nodded as if giving him permission to speak.

"We have a situation here, Dr. Good," Desmond said.

Sally wished he had better communications skills, but she thought she got the meaning he intended even if he was using cop-speak. To make sure, she said, "You mean there's something wrong?"

"That's right. We found the source of that e-mail about you."

"Then why the long faces? I thought that would be a good thing. We need to know who sent it so we can make sure there won't be any more like it."

"Well," Desmond said, "that's the trouble. We do know who sent it."

"Who was it?"

Desmond grimaced, as if his wedgie had been pulled even tighter.

"I'll let Ms. Gomez answer that one, I think."

Sally turned slightly so she could see Frankie better.

"Who sent it?" Sally asked.

"You did," Frankie told her.

Even when Frankie explained what had happened, Sally wasn't sure just how she'd managed to send an e-mail about herself, one that she hadn't written and had known nothing about. However, it seemed that Sally now had one more thing to blame on the Internet.

"There are certain kinds of services that specialize in anonymous e-mails," Frankie said. "Some of them are even located offshore, and they guarantee security. The sender's name and network information aren't shown in the message header. The sender can use a regular e-mail program like the one we use here at HCC to send the message through the secure server, and the recipients will have no idea where it came from."

"Then how do you know it came from my computer?"

"We started checking, and we found out that you had an account with one of those companies."

"But I don't."

"You might not know about it, but you have one. It's set up on your computer."

Sally shook her head, still not accepting

it, and sank back on the couch.

Desmond said, "You might remember that I've sent several memos to the whole faculty about locking office doors."

"And I've sent even more about the importance of password protection," Frankie said. "Do you leave your office door open and your computer turned on when you're in class or in a meeting?"

Sally admitted that she did.

"But nobody's ever stolen a thing," she said.

"You've been lucky," Desmond said. "I think Dr. Fieldstone should require everybody to lock their offices when they aren't there."

Sally was so dazed that she didn't even think about Desmond's pronoun problems. She had a much bigger problem of her own.

"This isn't like stealing," Frankie said. "But it's just as bad. Maybe worse. Your privacy has been invaded. I don't know why we haven't had something like this before." She paused. "Probably because nobody ever thought about it."

"What about requiring everybody to lock their offices?" Desmond said.

Fieldstone, who had kept quiet so far and seemed preoccupied, said, "I think it's a good idea. Security is more important than ever these days, especially computer security. I'll send a memo tomorrow, e-mail and hard copy."

Desmond nodded with satisfaction.

"What about finding the person who sent that e-mail?" Sally said.

"It would take a computer-savvy person to do something like send that e-mail," Desmond said.

"Not necessarily," Frankie said. "Just someone with a few basic skills. And I hope you're not suggesting that one of my staff had anything to do with it."

"I'm not," Desmond assured her. "I was thinking about a student. They seem to know a lot more about computers than most of us old guys do. Not just everybody would know about that secure e-mail service."

Frankie conceded the point, but she said that it was easy to find out about such things with a simple search.

"Students would know about all that, I'll bet," Desmond said.

Sally wondered again if Wayne Compton might have had something to do with the e-mail. She could check his records and see if he'd taken any computer courses. Not that it would prove anything if he had. Or hadn't. What had been done with the e-mail wasn't something that was taught in class.

"I don't suppose there's any way you could find out who set up that account," Sally said.

"No. It's funny that whoever it was left the information about the account on your computer, though. They didn't cover their tracks very well."

More pronoun problems. Sally thought it might be a good idea to invite Mr. Grammar Person to campus for a faculty seminar.

"Maybe they didn't want to cover their tracks," Desmond said. "Maybe they wanted us to think Dr. Good set up the account."

"That could be it," Frankie agreed. "But why?"

Sally couldn't figure out the why of any of it, but that was nothing new. She'd been puzzled all along.

"We'll find out why when we find the person who did it," Desmond said. "We'll just have to keep working on that. Meanwhile, if people will keep their offices locked, maybe it won't happen again."

"I hope that memo will include something about computer security and passwords," Frankie said. "I have to say, Dr. Good, that we inspected your computer this morning while you were out. Your office was wide open. Is it that way now?"

Sally wondered if the computer center staff thought it was fine for them to invade her privacy. She didn't see any difference between them and the person who'd sent the e-mail. Well, they weren't malicious. She'd give them that.

"My office is open, I'm afraid," she said.

"I thought you'd say that, and it's more convenient for us, I guess. We'd have needed to get a passkey from the police if it was locked."

"Why would you need to get into my office again?"

"We're taking your computer. We might be able to find something more if we can spend some time looking at your hard drive. Don't worry. We'll leave you another computer."

Sally felt a touch of panic. "But I have all my tests saved on that one. And all my assignments and student information plans. What about my privacy?"

"Surely you've backed everything up. You know that a hard drive can crash at any moment."

"I have most things backed up," Sally said.

She didn't add that she had a drawer full of little floppy disks but no idea what was on any particular one of them. She did have things saved, but finding them would be a real chore.

"Most things?" Frankie said.

"Just about everything. But I'd prefer to keep my computer. I'm not sure I like the idea of people snooping through my files."

"You haven't been downloading any pornography, have you?"

Sally smiled. "No, but I do get e-mail about penis enlargement."

Fieldstone cleared his throat. Desmond squirmed. Frankie smiled and said, "Don't we all. I promise you that we won't open any of your files. We're just going to check the computer for suspicious programs and look for a clue to the phantom e-mailer. We'll get the computer back to you as soon as we can. You really do need to be more careful about security from now on."

"I'll see that the memo emphasizes that," Fieldstone said. He stood up. "Dr. Good, I'd like for you to stay for a few minutes after the others leave."

Frankie and Desmond took that as their cue to go. Sally stayed on the couch, wondering what else Fieldstone could possibly want with her.

When the others had left and the door was safely closed behind them, Fieldstone told her.

15

When Jack got home that afternoon, Hector was waiting for him.

Hector was a cat. He wasn't exactly the cat Jack would have chosen if he'd been looking for an animal to live with him, but he hadn't been looking. The cat had just showed up one day, so beaten and bedraggled that he reminded Jack of the way Hector of ancient Troy must have looked after having been killed, tied to a chariot, and dragged three times around the walls of the city by the triumphant Achilles.

Jack, being a soft touch, had fed the scruffy cat, who must have approved of the gesture. He stayed at Jack's. He'd never become very friendly, but he'd proven to be courageous and a good cat to have around when Jack was in danger.

"You want to eat, right?" Jack said when he got out of his car.

Hector walked over to the food bowl in a corner of the garage without comment, and Jack poured some dry food out of a sack for him. Hector waited until Jack had put the sack down and watched him for a few seconds before he deigned to eat.

At first Jack had tried to persuade Hector that being a house cat was a good idea and that living inside was preferable to rambling around in the outdoors, but Hector had disagreed. He was never going to become domesticated if he could help it.

Jack left him to his meal and walked back out to the driveway to pick up his copy of the *Hughes Journal*.

For a long time, the *Hughes Weekly News* had been the only newspaper in town. Its name was something of a misnomer, as the paper had, until recently, rarely printed any actual news except of the most innocuous kind. Its purpose was to sell advertising, and as troublesome news or opinions might somehow offend an advertiser, none of that sort of thing had been allowed.

The publisher of the *Hughes Journal*, seeing an opportunity to offer the town something a little different, had started printing a weekly paper that was a bit livelier than the *Weekly News*. There were editorials in the *Journal*, and they were all considerably more contentious than anything that had ever appeared in the *Weekly*

News. The new paper was picking up advertising, so Jack assumed the editorials weren't bothering anyone. Maybe people even enjoyed them.

He went inside, tossed the paper on the kitchen table, and thought about what he could have for dinner. The little sandwich he'd had for lunch had been okay, but it had been awfully small. He was already hungry again, and it wasn't even four o'clock.

He looked in the freezer and found a Marie Callendar chicken potpie. He knew it contained about ten thousand fat grams, but he didn't care, because he also knew it would be tasty. Fat grams be damned. He wouldn't eat it at four o'clock, however. If he did, he'd be hungry yet again before time for bed. He'd read the *Journal*, which would take about two minutes, and then grade a few research papers before heating up the potpie.

Jack always staggered his research papers for the composition classes. Rather than have all the papers come in at once at the end of the semester, thus burying him beneath a ton of computer printouts, he always had one class do the paper early, with the others following at regular intervals during the course of the semester.

He'd have to boot up the computer to grade them. Although there were now services that promised to write original papers that would never be published on the Internet and never be resold, the papers were expensive. Jack had found that most students who wanted a canned paper went for one of the cheaper services. If he ran across a suspect paper, he Googled suspicious-sounding phrases. Often he located the original paper within minutes.

Word had gotten around about the Googling, and soon the paper services would figure a way around it. But for now Jack was satisfied that it worked well enough. And, to be fair, there were only a couple of students a year who didn't do their own work. Maybe the cheating was held to a minimum because someone had told the students that Jack and other HCC instructors were giving an automatic F in the course to anyone who used a plagiarized paper and that everything would be checked with a search engine. Well, to be honest about it, Jack told the students himself, every semester. He wanted to give them every chance to do the right thing. Some of them still tried to fool him, however, as if they were playing some sort of game. The ones he caught soon learned that what they thought was a game had serious consequences.

Jack went back out to the garage to check on Hector, who had already disappeared. He was somewhere nearby, Jack knew, lurking in the shrubbery, waiting to eviscerate some unsuspecting soul who happened by. Jack didn't often go outside at night for fear that Hector wouldn't recognize him. Jack had no desire to be eviscerated.

Back in the kitchen, Jack picked up the *Journal* and went into his den to read it. He flopped down in a chair, kicked off his Bass Weejuns, and opened the paper to the editorial, which was the thing he looked for first. It was usually the most interesting thing in the paper.

When he saw the title above the editorial, he unflopped, sitting up as rigid as if his backbone had suddenly fused into a bumpy skeletal rod. He read the title of the editorial again, then read it a third time.

Shaking his head, he went to the telephone.

It took Fieldstone a while to get around to what he wanted to say, and Sally waited impatiently. She wanted to go back to her

164

office and find out what kind of computer had been left there.

When Fieldstone finally got to the point, Sally came to attention.

"You're saying that Seepy Benton, Dr. Benton, I mean, was at Harold Curtin's house the night Curtin died?"

"That's right. I sent him there. I didn't know when he'd go, of course, and neither of us could have known what would happen after he left. I thought that Dr. Benton might be able to persuade Curtin that his opposition to the bond issue didn't make any sense."

"Did he?"

"No. Curtin was adamant about his position. Dr. Benton couldn't budge him."

"It's too bad that he had to visit Curtin on that particular evening," Sally said, wondering why Seepy hadn't said anything about his visit when he was talking to Jack. "Have you told the police that he was there?"

"No. That's what I wanted to ask you about. You know Detective Weems better than I do, and I thought you might be the one to talk to him."

Sally thought someone should have talked to Weems before now. Waiting to tell him that Benton had visited Curtin would just make Benton's actions seem suspicious.

"Lieutenant Weems isn't my biggest fan," Sally said. "Anyway, we don't know that Curtin's death was anything other than bad health. I don't think you should be worried."

"Don't the police find fingerprints? If they do, Dr. Benton's prints will be there in Curtin's apartment."

Sally knew where Curtin had lived. It was a small garage apartment that couldn't have had more than a couple of rooms, not exactly the kind of place she hoped to spend her last days. She could understand why Curtin had been bitter.

"It won't matter if they find fingerprints. In fact, they won't even look, not if Curtin wasn't murdered. But I think it would be a good idea if Weems were informed about the visit. Chief Desmond is the person to do it. He and Weems have worked together."

"Desmond was there, too."

"In Curtin's apartment? Desmond and Benton both? Together?"

Sally realized she was babbling, but she couldn't help it.

"Together," Fieldstone said. "It was a delicate situation."

"It's just a bond issue," Sally said in exasperation.

"No, it's more than that. Surely you've heard the rumors. Both Curtin and Larry Lawrence were going to run for the board if the bond was defeated. And they were going to try to get me fired."

"Wait a minute." Sally couldn't believe what she was hearing. "Larry Lawrence was there?"

Sally wondered how much Fieldstone knew about Desmond and Lawrence's daughter. If he knew what Sally had been told today, he should never have sent Desmond.

"It was an informal meeting," Fieldstone said, "but I wanted Desmond to be there in case there was any trouble. Mr. Talon was representing the board."

Sally almost strangled, but she managed to say, "Roy Don Talon was there?"

Fieldstone looked hurt at her tone. "I thought it would be good to have board representation."

Sally got control of herself. She said, "And was there trouble?"

"No. Words were exchanged. That's all."

"You're sure."

"There might have been a little shoving, but nothing more than that. As I understand it, Curtin had been drinking a bit. He's had something of a problem since he left us, you know. In fact, he might have been drinking more than a bit. He was functioning, but not very well, according to Dr. Benton."

"Good grief."

Fieldstone gave her an apologetic look. "You can see why I'm worried."

Sally could see, all right. She didn't blame him. When all this came out, and she was certain that it would, the college would be put in a bad light. People might be inclined to vote against the bond issue if they thought college administrators, board members, and police were trying to strong-arm the opposition.

"So will you talk to Weems?" Fieldstone said.

Sally sighed. Then she said she'd do what she could.

When Sally got back to her office, she had to get her key out of her purse to open the door. The first thing she saw was that her computer was gone. The replacement looked as if it had come out of a closet where it had been gathering dust and spiderwebs since 1995. She hoped it had a color monitor.

To calm herself, she finished grading the paper she'd started before Fieldstone had called. Then she went over to see Wynona Reed.

It was getting close to five o'clock. No one roamed the quiet halls. Most of the faculty had already left for the day, leaving only the secretaries and deans to occupy the building. In another hour or so people would be arriving for their evening classes, but at the moment the campus was quiet and almost deserted.

Wynona was working at her computer. Sally waited until she looked up.

"Has anybody been asking lately about getting an overhead projector moved to a room?" Sally asked.

Wynona scratched the side of her nose with a long red fingernail.

"You mean besides A. B. D. Johnson?"

"Yes. He's lost one, and I'm trying to find it."

"People move those things around all the time."

All the overheads sat on little carts that had signs attached to the side. The signs said, *This projector is not to be moved from Room ___*. The blank was filled in with the room number written in heavy black letters.

"I know people move them," Sally said. "They're not supposed to, but they do. I thought that if somebody had asked about one, you might remember."

"You could just go around and look in every room. I'll bet you a hundred dollars that not a single one is where it belongs."

Sally knew better than to take a bet from Wynona. She liked to visit the casinos in Louisiana and on the Indian reservation in east Texas. She was a consistent winner at the slots, or so people said.

"I thought you knew everything that goes on around here," Sally said.

"I do. You could probably figure out who took the overhead if you thought about it."

"I've thought about it. I don't have any idea."

"Anyone who'd take a stapler would take an overhead."

"Ellen?"

"Bingo. I could be wrong . . ." Wynona paused to let Sally think about how unlikely that would be. ". . . but she did come by the other day complaining that the bulb had burned out on the one in her room. She asked me to call media, but you know how that goes."

Sally knew. Sometimes it took a little

while to get a bulb replaced. Sometimes it took a long while.

"Thanks, Wynona. I knew you'd have the answer."

"See all, know all. If there's a skeleton in a closet, I can always rattle the bones."

"I believe it."

Sally left the office and walked down the deserted hallway to the classroom that Ellen Baldree preferred to teach in. Sure enough, there were two overhead projectors in the room. One belonged there, and one belonged in the room where A.B.D. taught. Sally rolled the cart to A.B.D.'s room and left it there. Maybe it would be there when he taught tomorrow. Maybe not.

When she got back to her office, she realized that she'd forgotten to close and lock the door. She'd have to focus better and try to remember to do that.

She looked at her telephone. The little red light was blinking to indicate that she had a message, but she didn't feel like talking to anyone. She'd check it tomorrow.

She locked the office and went home.

The light on Sally's home answering machine was blinking, too. She had a feeling

171

that she knew who'd called, but she checked the caller ID to be sure.

Her mother had called at 4:35, but there were several calls before that, all of them from Jack Neville. She wondered what Jack wanted. Whatever it was, it must have seemed urgent to him. She wished now that she'd checked her messages at the college.

Jack would have to wait. Sally would have to call her mother first. But not until she checked on Lola, who was lying in wait on the bed. When Sally came into the room, Lola jumped to the floor and started to scratch the rug.

"Stop that," Sally said.

Lola stopped and looked up at Sally for less than a second. Then she started to scratch the rug again.

"You're going to rip a hole in it," Sally said.

Lola gave her a look that implied complete disdain for the fate of the rug.

Sally decided that bribery was the way to go.

"How about a kitty treat?" she said.

Lola stopped scratching the rug and padded away to the kitchen. Sally trailed along behind her. She got a "hairball prevention" treat out and pitched it on the floor. Lola sucked it up and looked around for more.

"That's all there is," Sally told her, and Lola stalked back to the bedroom, tail in the air.

Sally needed a treat, too. She poured a glass of white wine and, feeling fortified, called her mother.

Editorial in the Hughes Journal

ARE THERE WITCHES IN OUR COLLEGE CLASSROOMS?

The *Hughes Journal* has learned that one of the instructors at Hughes Community College is distantly related to a witch named Sarah Good, who was convicted of the crime of witchcraft in Salem, Massachusetts, in 1692 and executed. Before her death, Sarah Good cursed her judges and promised one of them that "God would give him blood to drink." Two days ago, Harold Curtin, a former employee of the college who was an active opponent of the bond issue now before the citizens of the Hughes Community College district, died under suspicious circumstances, choking on his own blood. It would, of course, be irresponsible to suggest that there is any connection between the long-dead Sarah Good, her distant relative, and the death of Mr. Curtin, and the *Journal* draws no such conclusion.

However, it has been brought to our attention that there is an actual, practicing witch on the campus of HCC, a witch who, although unrelated to Sarah Good, had until recently a copy of a book about the pagan religion of Wicca on a desk in plain view. This situation begs several questions:

1. Is this the kind of instructor that we want for our college-age youth? A person who dances under the full moon at sabbats to celebrate the changing of the seasons?

2. Could it be that the current bond election has brought some kind of curse on those who are opposed to allowing the college a bigger percentage of our tax dollars?

3. Did Harold Curtin die of natural causes, or was something far more sinister at work?

The good people of our community deserve answers.

16

Sally's mother had psychic powers. Or so she claimed. She wasn't psychic in a general sense, which might have had some practical use. For example, Sally wouldn't have minded getting advance word about which Texas lotto numbers were going to be winners when the jackpot was somewhere up in the millions of dollars, but her mother didn't claim to be able to predict things like lotto numbers. Instead she claimed that she knew, or at least could sense, when someone in the family was in trouble. There was no use in telling her that such things were impossible. Sally had about as much chance of changing her mother's mind as she did of running a hundred yards with a refrigerator strapped to her back.

Her mother must have been waiting by the phone. She picked up on the first ring. Even her "hello" had an accusatory tone.

"You haven't called in a while," she said.

Sally held the receiver away from her head and took a sip of wine. When she'd swallowed it, she said, "I've been busy at the college."

"There's more to it than that. There's some kind of problem. I can sense it."

Maybe there was something to her mother's claims of clairvoyance after all. But even if that was true, Sally wasn't ready to admit it.

"The bond issue isn't going so well. Dr. Fieldstone has asked me to help out with a few things."

Sally thought it would be wise not to mention exactly what the "few things" were, and she certainly wasn't going to mention the e-mail about Sarah Good.

"Dr. Fieldstone is a shrewd man," her mother said. "You're by far the most capable person he has working for him."

Sally's mother had never met a single member of the HCC faculty, administration, or staff, but she wasn't the kind of person to let a little thing like that interfere with her right to express an opinion, which to her was not an opinion at all. It was an incontrovertible fact. So Sally didn't bother to contradict her.

"One of the bond's major opponents died the other night," Sally said.

"I had a premonition that something bad had happened. I didn't read anything about it in the *Houston Chronicle*, though. Were there suspicious circumstances? There seem to be a lot of those when people die in Hughes since you moved there. Some people have an aura that attracts danger, you know. You could be one of them."

"There's nothing suspicious going on," Sally said, though that wasn't strictly the truth. "And I don't attract danger. You don't have to worry about me."

"If you had any children, you wouldn't say that. A mother always worries, no matter how old her children get. It's just one of those things."

Sally drank the last of the wine. "Well, in this case, there's nothing to worry about. My classes are going well, I'm in good health, and Lola is feeling perky."

Lola had, in fact, returned to the kitchen. She was lying under the table, staring intently at a catnip mouse that she must have brought there earlier in the day. Sally reached down for the mouse's tail and gave it a tug. Lola lunged at the mouse, missed, and skidded a couple of feet on the kitchen tiles.

"You spoil that cat," Sally's mother said, harping on a familiar string.

"I know, but she's my cat."

Silence. Sally's mother was touchy. It was easy to hurt her feelings. The silence might have gone on for a while, but Sally heard the doorbell.

Lola heard it, too. She didn't like visitors and didn't welcome the interruption as much as Sally did. Grabbing her mouse in her mouth, she loped away toward the bedroom.

"Someone's at the front door," Sally told her mother as Lola disappeared from view.

"That's a weak excuse to stop talking to me."

"It's not an excuse. Listen."

Sally held up the phone. The doorbell rang again and again.

Sally's mother must have been able to hear it. She said, "You're doing that yourself."

"I wouldn't know how. I have to go now. I'll call you later."

"You don't have to do that."

It wasn't a whine, but there was a minute trace of self-pity.

"I want to," Sally said. "Good-bye."

Sally hung up the phone and went to the door. She opened it to find Jack and Vera standing there. Both of them were holding newspapers.

"Have you seen the *Journal* today?" Jack asked, waving his copy in her face.

Sally shook her head. "I haven't had time to look at it. I just got home a little while ago."

"You need to read it," Vera said, whacking the door frame with her copy.

Sally stepped aside and told them to come on in.

"We can have some wine while I read."

Jack looked at the empty glass in Sally's hand.

"Looks as if you have a head start."

"I needed it."

"You're going to need a whole bottle," Vera said as they followed her to the kitchen.

"Doesn't anybody know what 'begging the question' means any more?" Sally said when she looked up from the editorial.

They were sitting at Sally's kitchen table, each with a glass of wine and a newspaper.

"I'm glad you can joke about it," Vera said. "It shows you don't lose your composure easily."

"Either that or she's nuts," Jack said. "This is awful stuff."

"I agree," Sally said. "When an editorial

writer doesn't know how to use the language, we're headed down the road to hell in a handbasket."

"Ha. Ha," Jack said.

"Come on, Jack. Lighten up. You, too, Vera." Sally tapped the paper with her finger. "This sounds bad, but at least whoever wrote it had the sense not to name any names."

"It's just a matter of time before names are mentioned," Vera said. "Somebody has my book."

"I was wondering about that. How did anybody manage to get it? And how can anybody be sure it's yours?"

"It has my name in it."

"Now you're the one who's making jokes."

"I wish I were. But writing my name in my books is a habit with me, something I've done with every book I've owned since college. Whenever I get a book, I write my name inside the front cover."

"Well, that answers one of my questions," Sally said. "What about the other one?"

"You mean how did the newspaper get my book? I can't answer that. I wish I could."

"The editorial says it was on your desk."

"It wasn't, though. That's just not true. I would never leave it lying out in plain sight."

"But it was in her office at the college," Jack said.

"On the bookshelf," Vera said. "Not on the desk. This is terrible. Terrible."

Her voice was shaky. Sally had never heard Vera so unsure of herself.

"Let's all calm down," Sally said. "I don't see anything so terrible about it. Think it over. There's nothing in the least wrong with a college teacher having any kind of book at all on her shelves. You teach sociology, don't you, Vera? Why should anyone question the fact that you have a book on Wicca or anything else on your shelves? I'll bet you have books on Buddhism, Christianity, Hinduism, and a couple of other religions, too."

Vera's look of distress turned slowly to a grin.

"You're right. I do have a lot of books about religion and religious movements. They're all part of my library. I don't know why I didn't think of that."

"I do," Jack said. "You were too worried. And you were right to worry. Let's face it. People have a tendency to react emotionally when they read an editorial like that.

They don't sit down and think things over. *We* didn't even sit down and think it over."

Vera started to frown again. "So what are we going to do now that we have?"

"We're going to take the offensive," Sally said. "First of all, I'll call Christopher Matthys."

Vera brightened. "The school's attorney? Are we going to sue?"

"No, but we're going to have him call the paper and tell them what I just said about the books. Maybe throw in something about academic freedom."

"I think that's a great idea. Why don't you call the paper yourself?"

"It will sound better coming from a lawyer than from an English teacher. And I think I'll suggest that he say a few things about that ridiculous e-mail, too. Apparently even the newspaper got a copy. It's turned out to be a lot more than a joke."

"It was never a joke," Jack said. "It was meant to do some damage to your reputation and credibility. Did they find out yet who sent it?"

"I sent it," Sally said.

Vera and Jack both looked shocked.

"Just another little joke," Sally said, and then she told them what Frankie had found out.

"I always leave my door wide open, too," Jack said when she'd finished. "I always have. I never even gave it a second thought."

"I'm the same way," Vera said. "I've never lost a thing."

"Except that book," Sally reminded her. "Somebody took it from your shelves."

"I can't believe anyone would do that."

"Someone did, though," Jack said. "Things aren't as safe as they seem. From what Sally's told us, the computer center guys can even come into our offices, take our computers, and do with them as they will. Or search through them right there in the office if they want to do that."

"That's outrageous," Vera said. "We should take it up with the faculty senate."

"They aren't really *our* computers," Sally said. "They belong to the college. We're just using them."

"That still doesn't give anybody the right to take them and look at our files."

"Try telling that to Frankie Gomez or to Fieldstone."

Vera thought about that. "Maybe they have a point. Even if they don't, I'm getting us off the subject. We can worry about the computer issue later. When are you going to call Matthys?"

"Right now," Sally said.

"Calling him sounds like a good idea," Jack said. "But there's a problem with it. The *Journal* is a weekly paper. The next issue won't hit the driveways until next Tuesday. A lot can happen before then, even if they're willing to print some kind of retraction."

Sally knew he was right, but she didn't see what they could do about the delay, other than hope the editorial didn't stir up any trouble. She was afraid that was a vain hope.

"I'll call him anyway," Sally said. "It can't hurt, and I can't think of anything else."

"Might as well give it a try, then," Jack said, and Sally made the call.

Matthys, as it turned out, was already on the case.

"Dr. Fieldstone got in touch with me earlier," he told Sally. "As soon as he saw the editorial, in fact. He was irate. I thought he might have a heart attack while we were talking about it."

"The article's not libelous, is it?" Sally asked, hoping that he'd say *yes*.

"No, but it's irresponsible. It's full of innuendo and insinuations. I think we can make the paper's owner and his editorial writer pretty uncomfortable."

Sally didn't think *uncomfortable* was going far enough. She wanted the people responsible for the editorial to suffer some serious repercussions. She asked Matthys if he could at least get some kind of retraction and apology.

"I'll do my best. You can be sure of that. And here's another thing. The paper is in possession of stolen property. We can make an issue of that, too. Granted, it's not very valuable property, but it was stolen from an office, wasn't it?"

"Yes. Not from a desk, which is what the editorial said, but from some bookshelves."

"It doesn't matter where it came from, as long as it was stolen. Maybe we can scare them a little at the paper with that charge."

Scaring wasn't enough, either. Sally said, "Hang 'em high."

"Isn't that what they did to witches?"

"I take it back," Sally said.

"Good, because I don't think capital punishment will apply. Or even corporal punishment. All we can do is worry them and maybe get them to say they're sorry. But by the time we do, it might be too late."

Sally said they'd already thought of that. Then she thanked Matthys for whatever help he could give and hung up the phone. Then she told Jack and Vera what had been said.

"I'm sure people will behave rationally," she finished.

"Yeah, right," Jack said. "The way they always do. As for me, I wouldn't be surprised in the least if the peasants hadn't already armed themselves with shovels and pitchforks. If you look out your front windows, you might be able to see the torches moving up the street through the twilight."

Vera laughed and patted Jack's arm. "You really do have a vivid imagination."

"I stole it from a movie," Jack said.

"*Frankenstein*," Sally said.

"*Young Frankenstein*," Jack said, pronouncing the name *Frahnkensteen*. "That's the Mel Brooks version of the story, with Gene Wilder and Marty Feldman. I like Brooks's ending a lot better than the original."

" 'Oh sweet mystery of life,' " Vera said.

Though there was no wine left in Sally's glass, she lifted it as if in a toast and said, "To happy endings."

"Hear, hear," Jack said, "and the sooner, the better."

He and Vera clicked their empty glasses against Sally's.

"Is making a toast with an empty glass bad luck?" Vera asked.

Sally said she didn't know, and that was when they heard the chanting from outside.

17

Standing in front of Sally's house was a group of people carrying signs that identified them as members of Mothers Against Witchcraft. Or, as one of them proclaimed, *Mother's Against Witchcraft.*

The use of the apostrophe was a dying art, Sally thought as she looked out over the crowd of eight or ten people, all but one of them women. The Mothers Against Witchcraft didn't attract a big membership.

The members, however, made up in noise what they lacked in numbers. They brandished homemade signs painted on posterboard and nailed to thin sticks of wood as they chanted, "Witches get out! Witches get out!"

Sally was glad to see that nobody was carrying a pitchfork or a torch.

The leader of the mob, if such a small group could be called a mob, was, of course, Jennifer Jackson. Her sign said, *Get the Witches Out of Our School!* Another woman carried one that said, *Witch's Don't Belong at HCC!*

Sally sighed. They really could use some help with their sign-making, not that she intended to volunteer.

The only man in the group was Sherm Jackson. He didn't have a sign, and he stood well behind the others, as if he hoped no one would notice him.

Sally was disappointed in both of them, not that she'd expected anything better. Still, after she'd explained about the e-mail, about her nonexistent relationship with Sarah Good, and about libel and slander, she'd hoped Jennifer would let things drop.

She should have known better. Jennifer wasn't going to let the facts interfere with what she believed to be true. Sally was getting more and more students like that in her classes. They were always sure that whatever they believed was the truth, and no amount of proof to the contrary could change their minds. If they believed it, it was true to them, and therefore it should be true for everyone. Ralph Waldo Emerson would have been proud of them. But Sally just found them irritating. Maybe they reminded her of her mother.

Sally waited in her doorway, looking

from one woman to the other, the way she looked at chatty students in a classroom, not saying a word herself, just waiting patiently until the noise died away.

It was a technique that had served her well in the past, and it worked just as well there at her house as it did in class. The chanting began to decrease in volume until Jennifer Jackson was the only one whose lips were still moving, and very little sound was coming out of her mouth.

Sally waited until there was no noise at all except for the sound of a car driving down the street a block away. Then she said, "Good evening. I don't know what you think you're doing here, but I'd appreciate it if you'd get out of my yard and go back home."

Jennifer raised and lowered her sign.

"Witches get out!" she said.

Another woman echoed her, but not very enthusiastically, and no one else joined them.

Sally didn't say anything. She just stood there and looked from one face to the other as if she might be memorizing each one. The women began to give one another uneasy glances. Sally knew they were beginning to have doubts about what they were doing, and she thought they would have left within a few minutes if Vera hadn't appeared beside her.

"There's the other one!" Jennifer said. She pumped her sign up and down. "They're together, having one of their witch meetings! Witches get out! Witches get out!"

Encouraged by her sudden animation, the other women joined her, and the chanting resumed.

Sally could see that a few porch lights were on at houses up and down the street. Her neighbors were standing outside and trying to see what all the commotion was.

"I'm sorry," Vera said. "I thought I might be able to help, but it looks as if I just got them cranked up again."

"Don't say anything," Sally told her. "Just look at them."

Vera caught on quickly. She'd been a teacher for as long as Sally had, and she knew how to deal with unruly students. She stood beside Sally without moving anything other than her eyes, which roved over the small crowd. Sally had to admire her impassivity, which was even more practiced than Sally's own.

It took a bit longer this time, but after a while the volume of the chanting got lower and lower until Jennifer was carrying on alone. Then she stopped, too.

"You're trespassing on my property, you know," Sally said into the silence.

It was getting closer to dark now, but she could still see Jennifer's thin, intense face. Her eyes were as brilliant as if she had a fever.

"If you're not gone in two minutes," Sally said, "I'm going to go back inside and call the police."

"We're within our rights to be here," Jennifer said.

Sally wondered who was giving her such bad legal advice. She wished she had her Ladysmith. If she fired a couple of shots over their heads, even Jennifer might change her mind.

Or she might have a stroke.

Or the bullet would hit an innocent by-stander a few blocks away.

As satisfying as it would be to see Jennifer Jackson's face as Sally pulled out her roscoe and blazed away, it was better to leave the pistol right where it was.

"We don't want witches teaching at our college," Jennifer said. "When you resign, we'll leave."

"You're going to get very hungry out in my yard if you wait for me to resign. And the dew is awfully uncomfortable in the mornings."

Jennifer thought that over for a while.

"We'll leave now, but we'll be back. You can't corrupt the youth of our town anymore with your satanic ideas."

Sally hoped Vera would keep quiet. This was no time for a lecture about the fact that Satan didn't figure into the religion of Wicca.

Vera took a deep breath, and Sally nudged her with an elbow. Vera let out the breath slowly and said nothing.

"The thing is," Sally said, "that there are no witches here, and there are no witches teaching at HCC. You're mistaken about that, even though you don't seem able to admit it."

Jennifer pointed her sign at Vera.

"We know about that woman's pagan book. You can't deny that it exists and that it belonged to her."

"Yes, and whoever stole it could be arrested for theft," Sally said. "Besides, Ms. Vaughn owns quite a few books on different religions."

Jennifer gave her cohorts a triumphant look, and Sally realized her mistake. To Jennifer, to own a book written about any religion other than Christianity was probably just as heinous a crime as being a witch.

"They're for the courses she teaches," Sally said, and then she clamped her mouth shut as she realized that was the worst possible thing she could have said.

"Corrupting our kids!" Jennifer said, pumping her sign. "Witches get out! Witches get out!"

"There they go again," Vera said.

"Sorry. I made the mistake of thinking we were dealing with rational people."

Jennifer put down her sign and picked up a cloth carryall that had been sitting at her feet. She reached in and brought out something that Sally couldn't quite see. Then she threw it, and an egg splattered on the side of Sally's house.

"She's a total bitch," Vera said, "and she throws like a girl."

"Which is a good thing," Sally said, as another egg hit the wall not far away.

"Are we going to stand out here and get egged?" Vera asked. "Or are we going out there in the yard and beat the crap out of them?"

Sally wasn't sure that was a good idea.

"There are a lot more of them than there are of us. And we'd be lowering ourselves to their level."

Vera shrugged. "As if I cared about that."

"What about Jack? We could use a little help since we're so outnumbered."

Vera looked over her shoulder. "He was right here a second ago. I don't know where he went."

She sounded a little disappointed, as she'd expected Jack to be at least as macho as she was.

"Maybe he had to use the bathroom," Sally said.

"Maybe he's just a coward."

Sally thought about some of the things she'd been through with Jack.

"He might not be Sir Galahad," she said, "but he's no coward."

Another egg hit the wall, much closer this time.

"She's getting better," Vera said. "If we're going to take them on, now's the time."

"Do you want to call Jack?"

"Two tough chicks like us? I don't think we really need him, do you?"

"No," Sally said. "Let's go beat the crap out of them."

So they went out into the yard to do just that.

18

"Jennifer Jackson is mine," Sally said as they stepped out of the house. "Do you have any favorites?"

"I'll take whoever I can get," Vera told her.

The Mothers Against Witchcraft appeared somewhat alarmed when Sally and Vera began to advance on them. They all retreated a few steps, except for Jennifer, who held her ground.

And she held her sign, too, brandishing it like a club.

"You'd better stay away from me," she said. "I have a right to defend myself."

"You need to get a lawyer, just to make sure," Sally said.

She grabbed the posterboard and gave it a jerk. Jennifer was so surprised that she let go of the sign. Sally dropped it to the ground and stepped on it.

"Get off my property," she said. "Before you get hurt."

"I'll sue you for assault!"

"I haven't assaulted you yet. But I'm thinking about it."

While she was thinking about it, Sally looked for Vera, who, as Sally might have guessed if she'd tried, was shoving her way through the other women to get to Sherm Jackson. Leave it to Vera to go for the man.

The women weren't trying to stop her. They were mostly just getting out of her way. Sally didn't think they'd expected a fight.

Instead of looking for Vera, Sally should have kept her eyes on Jennifer, who reached down for the sign. She grabbed hold of the stick and wrenched the sign from beneath Sally's feet, throwing Sally off balance.

As Sally stumbled backward, Jennifer swung the sign like a baseball bat and hit Sally in the side.

It didn't hurt, since the posterboard had too much wind resistance to allow Jennifer to make an effective swing, and the sign didn't weigh much anyway. But it made Sally angry. Until that moment, she had been perfectly calm, but getting hit by the sign put her over the line.

For just a second she wished that she were a real witch, one with the power to give Jennifer Jackson blood to drink. Since that wasn't possible, she did what she thought was the next best thing.

She stepped up to Jennifer and punched her in the stomach.

It wasn't much of a punch, but it took Jennifer completely by surprise. Her mouth made an *O* of shock. She dropped her sign and staggered for two steps before sitting down on the ground. Hard.

Sally, who was almost as surprised as Jennifer, recovered more quickly. She picked up the sign and snapped the stick in two over her knee. She tossed the pieces to the ground and gave the other women a who-wants-a-piece-of-me-next look.

Nobody did. The women were all backing away, trying to escape. A couple were already getting into one of the cars parked at Sally's curb.

Then Sally saw Vera, who was boxing Sherm Jackson's ears.

Sherm wasn't trying to fight back, and he wasn't doing much to defend himself, either. Vera seemed to be having a wonderful time, and she might have kept it up forever if it hadn't been for the sirens.

Sally heard them faintly at first, but they rapidly increased in volume. As they did, the Mothers Against Witchcraft moved more quickly, dumping their signs and jumping into cars. In less than a minute, two police cars turned the corner and came squealing to a stop, but the Mothers were one step ahead. Three carloads of women peeled away from the curb at almost the same moment the police cars' sirens started winding down.

In fact, only two Mothers remained, Jennifer and her husband, and Sally wasn't really sure that a man could be counted as a mother. Well, she supposed it was possible, metaphorically speaking.

Sherm stood in front of Vera not saying a word. He looked dejected, as well he might, considering how Vera had boxed his ears.

Jennifer sat on the grass, still panting a little as if she couldn't quite catch her breath. Sally allowed herself a small grin. She knew it was wrong to feel good about what she'd done, but she couldn't help herself.

She stopped grinning when the uniformed cops reached her. They didn't look happy.

"All right, what's going on here?" one of them said.

"Trespassers," Sally told him. "I was trying to get them out of my yard. They wouldn't go, and one of them" — she pointed to Jennifer — "hit me with that sign."

The cop picked up the half of the sign that had the posterboard on it, turned it over, and read it aloud.

"Mothers against witchcraft," he said. "What's that?"

Sally didn't think she could explain it, but she didn't have to. Another car arrived at the curb, and Lieutenant Weems got out.

He walked over to Sally, shaking his head. Then he looked up at the darkening sky.

"Why me, Lord?" he said.

Sally didn't even try to answer that one. He wasn't talking to her, anyway.

"Are you going to file any charges?" he asked Sally after his brief communication with the sky.

She was about to tell him that she hadn't given any thought to what she was going to do, but he didn't let her speak.

"No," he said, "you're not." He looked down at Jennifer. He didn't offer to help her get up. "And you aren't, either. Get your sign and get out of here."

Jennifer stood up with an exaggerated look of pain and annoyance. The cop handed her the sign, and she picked up the other piece of it. Clutching the pieces to her chest, she stalked over to join Sherm, who was now looking more sheepish than dejected. They didn't speak. They just got into their SUV and drove away.

There were still several abandoned signs lying in the yard. Sally wondered if the Mothers could be arrested for littering, but she didn't think this was the time to ask.

Vera came over to stand by Sally and punched her upper arm.

"I guess we showed those candy asses," she said.

Clearly she felt no guilt about having taken advantage of Sherm. Sally found that she wasn't sorry for hitting Jennifer, either.

Weems sent the other cops away. When they'd left, he joined Sally and Vera.

"You two are a lot of trouble. I shouldn't have come, but I figured I owed Neville a favor."

"You gave me the third degree," Jack said, coming out of the house. "Coming over here was the least you could do to pay me back for my pain and suffering."

"There wasn't any pain. And anyway I apologized for that."

"Not exactly. I don't think you ever said 'I'm sorry.'"

"And I'm not going to say it, either," Weems told him. "I was just doing my job."

Vera said, "That's what all the jackbooted fascists say."

Sally didn't know if she was joking or not.

Weems looked Vera over. "I'm beginning to be sorry I came to help you out. I should have let those uniform boys haul you off to the jail for the night. A few hours in the tank might have changed your attitudes. And it would have served you right."

"I'd like to see you try hauling me off," Vera said.

"Yeah," Jack said. "You should have seen her whipping up on old Sherm Jackson."

"I'll pretend I didn't hear that, just in case the gentleman decides to file assault charges."

Sally wondered why the police always referred to criminals as *gentlemen* and *ladies*. It had always seemed odd to her that when a police spokesman was being interviewed on TV, he would say something like, "The gentleman we're looking for has already shot two people tonight, and we consider him very dangerous." Or, "The lady stabbed her husband thirty-five times."

Sally didn't regard shooting people as gentlemanly behavior, nor did she consider stabbing a particularly ladylike activity, but maybe she just wasn't being politically correct.

"Nobody's going to file assault charges against me," Vera said. "And if he does, I'll kick his butt."

"I'll pretend I didn't hear that, either," Weems said. "But that's it. If I ever owed you a favor, Neville, it's taken care of. We're even."

Jack nodded. "If you say so."

"I just did. I have a lot more to worry about than some little neighborhood rumble, and I'm afraid the three of you might be mixed up in it."

Sally didn't like the sound of that one little bit.

"What are you talking about?" she said.

"You don't really want to hear it, but I'll tell you this much. Your friends who just left will love it if you're implicated."

That sounded even worse.

"Don't play games with us," Sally said. "We have a right to know what you're talking about if you think it has something to do with us."

"Maybe you do have a right, at that. I guess I can tell you. You'll be reading about it in the paper tomorrow anyway. You remember your friend Curtin?"

"How could we forget?" Jack said. "But he wasn't our friend."

"Yeah," Weems said. "I know that. I also know that he didn't die of natural causes."

Sally had been afraid that might be what Weems had to tell them.

"How did he die, then?"

"It wasn't a curse, if that's what you're wondering. Maybe it was supposed to look that way, but thanks to some smart police work, we figured it out."

"Figured what out?"

"That Curtin was poisoned," Weems said.

19

Sally never missed a class unless there were compelling reasons why she should. In her entire teaching career, she had missed exactly one day of school because of illness, though she had missed more than that in order to attend conventions or teachers' meetings that were held out of town. In those cases she had always found someone to take her classes for her and either teach the assignment or give a test.

But on the day after the *Journal* editorial, she seriously considered giving her American literature class a walk. She just didn't feel up to going into the room and facing Wayne Compton and the rest of the students. She might have stayed in her office with her door closed if Vera hadn't come by and given her a pep talk.

"You can't hide in here and eat Hershey bars forever," Vera said. "Although I have to admit it's an attractive idea."

"How did you know about the Hershey bars?" Sally asked.

She'd thought the candy was a secret from everyone except Eva. After all, keeping candy, and for that matter any other kind of food, in the office had been expressly forbidden by order of Dean Naylor, who claimed that it attracted roaches and ants. Sally didn't believe it, so she ignored the order.

"Everybody knows about your Hershey bar habit. Your office is practically right across from Wynona's, and you never close your door."

Sees all, knows all, Sally thought.

"I should have known. Have you forgiven Jack for calling the police last night?"

"I'm going to let him suffer for a little while longer. We didn't need the cops. We had that bunch of wimps on the run."

Sally had to admit that Vera was right about that, but she felt she had to defend Jack.

"He was just trying to help."

"If he wanted to help, he could have come out in the yard and done some of the fighting."

"Not that we needed him," Sally said, and Vera laughed.

"No, and he did the sensible thing. I'll forgive him later today."

She went off to get ready for her own

class, and Sally sat at her desk and tried to concentrate on what she was going to say about Poe's "Berenice." She liked to approach it as a story of vampirism, having recently read an article on the topic by two professors named Blythe and Sweet. It had appeared in *Poe Studies,* and Sally had found it convincing. But it wasn't easy to think about fictional vampires when there was a real murder to be considered.

From what she had been able to coax out of Weems after he'd told her that Curtin had been poisoned, Sally gathered that Curtin had been drinking more than a little the evening of his death. He might not have been falling-down drunk, but he was close to that point. He was so drunk, in fact, that he never noticed when someone slipped a glass filled with poison into his hand.

Except that it wasn't really poison. It was what Weems had called a "cationic detergent."

"Like fabric softener," he'd said.

"You mean that stuff is poison?" Jack had asked. "I use it in my laundry."

"Yeah, but you aren't drinking it. And you'd need quite a bit of it, or a more concentrated solution, to kill yourself. It can wreck your esophagus and cause vomiting, which is what happened to Curtin. That's where the blood came from, not from any curse. Someone wanted us to think it had to do with witchcraft. Maybe trying to throw us off the track."

That last remark had made Sally feel a little better, and she asked about the time of death. Weems had given her a puzzled look, as if wondering why she wanted to know, but Sally didn't think it would be a good idea to tell him that several people from the college had been at a meeting with Curtin the evening he'd died, even if Fieldstone had asked her to do it. Now wasn't the time. So she told him she was just curious.

"We haven't established the time yet. But we will. You can count on that."

"How do you know he didn't kill himself?"

"It's a possibility. But there was no note, and it didn't look like an accident."

Sally had a few more questions, but Weems had left without giving out any more information.

Now Sally was trying to figure out what it all meant. She couldn't imagine Desmond or even Roy Don Talon slipping somebody a glass of fabric softener. They were more direct types. Roy Don would want a shoot-out on Main Street, and Desmond would probably prefer the same.

Seepy Benton was another story. He wasn't the macho type, and poison might just be his weapon of choice, that is, if he ever chose to kill somebody. Sally thought it might be a good idea to talk to him, so she picked up her phone and called his office. Molly Evans answered, and when Sally asked about an appointment, Molly told her to come on by whenever she felt like it.

"Dr. Benton will be in the office all morning. He's working on some kind of statistical analysis of the faculty salaries in the Gulf Coast–area colleges. It's not a lot of fun, and Dr. Benton would be glad for a break."

Sally said she'd come by after class. She hung up and got her books together, hoping she could get through a discussion of "Berenice" without having to answer any questions about editorials in the local newspaper.

As it turned out, she could. She should have known that hardly any of her students read the paper. If they got any news at all, they got it from television. And if their parents read the paper, they didn't discuss it with their offspring.

Sally gave a pop quiz on the story, handled Wayne's questions as best she could, and then launched into a discussion of "Berenice." Several of the students seemed fascinated with the idea that it might be about vampirism, and one of them even asked if vampirism figured into "The Fall of the House of Usher."

"That Madeline is pretty creepy," the student said.

"That's an excellent observation," Sally told him, amazed that someone was reading ahead, "and that's what we'll be talking about on Friday. Please read the story very carefully if you haven't already, and keep in mind what we've discussed today."

Several people stayed after class for a few minutes to talk about one thing or another — vampires, research papers, their grades — so Sally was a little later in getting to Seepy Benton's office than she'd planned. It didn't matter, however, as Molly waved her on in as soon as she arrived.

"He hasn't even taken a coffee break," Molly said. "He's dedicated to his job."

Sally went into the office, only slightly daunted by the coonskin cap and whip that hung on the coatrack.

"About that whip," Molly called. "I want you to know that my relationship with Dr. Benton is strictly professional."

"I never doubted it for a second," Sally said.

"The guitar is the most dangerous weapon in there," Molly said. "Don't let him get his hands on it."

Seepy Benton looked up from the pile of papers on his desk and smiled.

"She complains a lot, but she loves my music. I wrote a new song last night. It's called 'Friends Don't Let Friends Vote Republican.' Want to hear it?"

"No," Molly said from the outer office. "We don't. Not again. Spare me."

"What a kidder," Seepy said. "Just let me get my guitar, and I'll sing it for you."

"I don't really have time," Sally said.

She didn't want to be ungracious, but she wasn't in the mood for a song.

Seepy gazed at her sadly.

"It's too bad that none of the English teachers appreciate poetry," he said. "Jack Neville felt the same way about listening to my songs."

"It's not that I don't want to hear the song. It's just that I have other things on my mind. I need to talk to you about your meeting with Harold Curtin. The one that

Roy Don Talon and Eric Desmond went to with you."

Seepy leaned back in his chair. "Oh. That one."

"Yes," Sally said. "I think you forgot to mention it to Jack when he came by yesterday."

Seepy leaned forward. "Molly, why don't you take a break. Go to the cafeteria and have some of that good frozen yogurt."

"I know when I'm not wanted," Molly said. "But I'll be back in half an hour. You can sing after I leave if you want to. I don't mind."

She left, and when the outer door closed, Seepy said, "I thought that meeting was a secret."

"Not from me," Sally said. "Dr. Fieldstone told me about it. I think you and he should get Desmond to tell Weems that you were there at Curtin's apartment that night, especially now that we know Curtin has been murdered."

Seepy's eyes widened. "I wasn't aware that we knew that."

"It was supposed to be in the Houston paper today, but I don't know if it was."

Sally hadn't taken the time to read the paper that morning. She'd had to call her mother, having forgotten to call her back

212

after the episode with the Mothers Against Witchcraft. The call had taken a full twenty minutes, with Sally escaping only by claiming that it was time for her to leave for the college.

"I didn't see anything about it," Seepy said. "But I wasn't looking. It could have slipped by me."

"I expect that Dr. Fieldstone would have called you if it had been in there. He might not know yet, himself. Maybe we should go tell him."

Seepy didn't like that idea, but Sally made him see the wisdom of it. He called Eva Dillon and told her that he needed to see Fieldstone.

"Something important has come up," he said.

He listened for a second, then hung up.

"She said that Dr. Fieldstone would see me as soon as I could get there." He stood up and went over to the coatrack. "I might need my bullwhip for this meeting."

Sally didn't think so. She thought he'd need an asbestos suit instead of the black-and-gold Hawaiian shirt he was wearing.

"Leave the whip. You can wear the cap if you want to."

"I could, at that. It makes me feel like a rugged frontiersman."

Sally couldn't believe he was actually considering it.

"On second thought," she said, "forget it. Let's go."

They left the office, but Seepy gave a wistful look over his shoulder at the cap and whip as they went out the door.

Fieldstone had heard the news about Curtin from Eric Desmond, who was waiting in Fieldstone's office when they got there.

"This is serious," Fieldstone said. "We could have a little public relations problem with this."

Sally thought that it was a lot more than a little public relations problem. Harold Curtin had been murdered, after all, and he might have been killed by one of the four people in the room. Or by a board member, Roy Don Talon. There was nothing "little" about the problems that could come from that.

"We didn't kill Harold Curtin, if that's what you're worried about," Seepy told Fieldstone. "Roy Don, Chief Desmond, and I can each serve as an alibi for the others. We were all together, and I can swear that none of us killed him."

"He was poisoned," Desmond said. "I

talked to Weems this morning."

"And you didn't tell him you'd been there?" Sally said.

She knew it was a mistake to imply criticism of the chief, but she couldn't help herself. It just slipped out.

"I didn't tell him," Desmond admitted. "I thought it would look bad to tell him at this late date. We should have told him sooner."

"I didn't want him to tell," Fieldstone said, in a rare instance of taking the blame. "I thought it would reflect poorly on the school if word about the meeting got out. Now I know I was wrong and that keeping quiet is only going to cause more problems. We have to deal with this right now, before it gets any worse." He stopped to look at Sally. "I asked Dr. Good to tell Weems about the meeting, but apparently she hasn't gotten around to it yet."

"I had other things to worry about," Sally said.

"Yes, I suppose that's true. That editorial in the *Journal* was terrible. I've talked to Christopher Matthys about it, and he's going to try to get the paper to print a retraction and an apology. He's threatening them with a lawsuit, but we don't really have grounds for one. The best thing I can say about the editorial is that when people find out Curtin was murdered, they'll forget about the witches who teach here."

"No witches teach here," Sally said.

"What about that book? The one on Wicca?"

"Anybody can own a book. The only people who object are the Mothers Against Witchcraft, and there aren't that many of them."

"They're vocal, though. Very vocal."

"Their leader was also working with Curtin," Seepy said. "Jennifer Jackson. Tell him about what we saw, Chief."

"We saw a car just as we were leaving Curtin's apartment," Desmond said. "It pulled up to the curb not far from us. Dr. Benton mentioned it at the time, but I didn't think anything of it. Now I do, because Roy Don Talon said that Sherm Jackson drives one just like it."

"So what?" Fieldstone said.

"So maybe he or his wife had a meeting with Curtin after we did."

"Exactly what happened at your meeting?" Sally said. "Dr. Fieldstone said words were exchanged and that things got rough."

"It wasn't like that," Seepy said. "We might have raised our voices a little, but Curtin was drunk. He was doing most of the yelling. He said some things he shouldn't have, about Larry Lawrence."

Fieldstone looked at Desmond, and Sally realized that he'd heard the stories about Lawrence's daughter.

"They were personal things," Seepy went on. "They had nothing to do with what we'd gone there to discuss. Curtin was drunk, but he still shouldn't have said them."

"He had a right," Desmond said. "I behaved badly with Linda Lawrence, and Larry's very upset about it. I've tried to help out, but he won't hear of it. He's determined to hurt the college if he can, and it's my fault. I'm trying to work things out with Linda, and things are a lot better between us. I've gotten her some help for her problems, and she's almost straightened out. Not that Larry cares."

"And it's none of Curtin's business," Seepy said. "He was out of bounds. But even with the yelling, there was no rough stuff. Curtin tried to stand up once, and he fell down. I helped him back into his chair. That's all that happened."

Sally wondered if they were telling the truth. They'd had time to get together and concoct whatever story they wanted to tell. Still, Desmond sounded genuinely sorry about Linda Lawrence, and maybe he really was trying to do the right thing.

"Anyway," Seepy said, "we didn't kill anybody. And as I was saying before we got off the track, I'm sure that one of the Jacksons was there at Curtin's after we left. Maybe both of them."

"To discuss the bond issue, do you think?" Sally said.

"Maybe," Seepy said. "But Curtin was alive when we left. Maybe they're the ones who killed him."

"Then Weems has to be told."

"I know," Desmond said. "I'll talk to him."

"You do that," Fieldstone said. "Right now."

20

Troy Beauchamp was waiting for Sally outside her locked office door.

"I see you got the memo," he said, tapping on the door.

"Yes," Sally said.

She didn't want to hurt his feelings by telling him that she'd known about the memo before it had even been written. She handed her books to Troy, who held them while she got the key from her purse and unlocked the door. They went into the office and Sally told him to put the books on her desk.

"Anywhere you can find a spot," she said.

Troy looked around for a couple of seconds before saying there wasn't a spot.

Sally took the books and put them on a precarious stack of papers. When the stack started to slide, she stopped it and jiggled it around.

"Stay right there," she said, and it did. Maybe she was a witch after all.

Troy was fairly bouncing on his toes with

eagerness by that time. He must have had some big news.

"So, Troy, what's going on?" Sally said to give him his opening.

"Harold Curtin was murdered!"

Let him have his fun, Sally thought. She said, "No! Really?"

"Poisoned," Troy said. "I heard Chief Desmond saying something about it to one of the other cops."

"Then I'm off the hook."

"That's right. But did you read that editorial in the *Journal*?"

Sally said that she had.

"Those swine. I wonder who they could be talking about. Besides you, that is."

If he didn't know, Sally wasn't going to be the one to tell him.

"It doesn't matter. Anyone could have a book about Wicca in her office. Or his office. Even you."

"I don't, though."

"What about Greek religion? You teach the world literature course. You must have something about the Greek gods."

"Well, of course. But that's not like witchcraft."

"Sure it is. There's Medea, for example. But the whole system is pagan and contrary to the beliefs of all our students. I've even had complaints about it, as I'm sure you remember."

"Oh," Troy said. "Yeah."

It had been one of Troy's students who had complained about the content of the world literature course. He'd said he couldn't possibly read the assignments from the section of the book that dealt with Greek and Roman literature because they conflicted with his religious beliefs. Sally had told him to take British literature instead.

"I should have thought about that," Troy said.

"That's right. So don't worry about any books that people might have in their offices. People are going to be offended by something. If there's nothing to be offended by, they'll make up something."

"I'm offended by math books."

Sally laughed and said that she was, too.

"I wonder if some offended student killed Harold," Troy said.

"I don't think so," Sally said, "but you never know."

Troy agreed and left the office. Sally tried to arrange things on her desk so that there wouldn't be a paper-and-book cascade if she made any sudden moves. When things looked stable, she sat down and tried to think through all that had happened. Maybe somewhere along the way she'd missed the clue that would pull everything together.

She couldn't think of any reason why the Jacksons would kill the Garden Gnome. They were on his side, supposedly. The fact that he was drunk could have figured into it, but Sally didn't know how.

So if the Jacksons hadn't killed him, and Fieldstone's delegation from the college hadn't, then who had?

Sally gave it up and started to wonder about other things. The e-mail about her, for one. Who would do a thing like that?

The answer came to her almost immediately. It had been there all along, and she felt foolish for not having thought of it at the beginning.

Well, she thought, it wasn't the clue to the whole shebang, and it might not even be a clue at all, but she should never have overlooked something so obvious.

There was always a chance that she could be wrong, but she knew it would be easy enough to check. Wynona would know the answer to Sally's question.

"Ellen Baldree?" Wynona said when Sally asked. "Sure. She was in your office a couple of times when you were in class. I thought she was 'borrowing' a book. You know, the way she 'borrowed' that stapler and that overhead projector."

Sally figured Wynona was wrong. Ellen had been in the office to use Sally's computer. She had the skills, and her resentment against Sally had been building for a long time now with no relief. Sending out an e-mail that would cause Sally some trouble might be just the kind of thing Ellen would do.

"Should I have told you she was in there?" Wynona asked. "I didn't think anything of it. Is she the reason we got that memo about locking our doors and creating a password for everything?"

"Maybe," Sally said. "I'm about to find out."

"How?"

"I'm going to ask her."

"I don't think so," Wynona said. "She's not here."

"Not here? Where is she, then?"

"That's a good question. A student from her nine o'clock class came by around nine-thirty and asked me the same thing. She didn't show up for class."

That wasn't like Ellen at all, Sally thought. She might have resented Sally, but she was as dedicated to meeting her classes as Sally was. She'd never missed one before, at least not since Sally had been the department chair.

"You should have told me."

"I was going to, but you were in class, and then you didn't come back. I got busy. Anyway, I thought you knew. Faculty members are supposed to call their department chairs if they're not going to be here."

"She didn't call me. Check her schedule and see when her next class is. You meet it if she's not here, and tell the students that Ms. Baldree will be back on Friday."

"How do you know that she will?"

"I don't, but she'd better be here if she wants to keep her job. I'm going to call her right now."

Sally went back to her office and checked the answering machine just to be sure there were no messages from Ellen. There weren't, so Sally dug out the faculty directory and called Ellen's home phone number. No answer. Sally left a message on the answering machine. Then she did some more thinking.

Jack Neville was so worried that he couldn't even concentrate on his Spider

Solitaire game. Of all the things he had on his mind, Vera worried him the most. She was treating him as if he were some kind of sniveling coward just because he'd called the police at Sally's place. He'd tried to explain that he wasn't going to beat up on a bunch of women just to impress her, but she'd paid him no mind.

And he was worried about the calls he'd occasionally received from the Garden Gnome. It was almost as if Curtin had been trying to recruit him for the Citizens for Fiscal Responsibility. What would have given him the idea that a faculty member would join a group like that? Had someone told Curtin that Jack might be interested?

He looked at his watch. It was almost noon. Maybe Sally would like to go to lunch with him. If she did maybe Vera would be jealous enough to forgive him.

Almost as soon as he had the thought, he was ashamed of himself. It was an example of how low he had sunk that he would consider using Sally to make Vera jealous. Besides, he didn't really think it would work. Vera wasn't the jealous type.

He wasn't sure what type she was, in fact. He was still amazed that somehow they'd gotten together. They'd known each other for years, and they'd certainly never been friendly during that time. They'd hardly even spoken to one another except in passing when they were in the mail room or on the way to a class. But now that they had a relationship, he didn't want it to end.

He wondered if there might be some feat of bravery he could perform to impress Vera, but if there was, he didn't know what it could be. Anything he could do, she could do better.

To take his mind off things, he switched from Spider Solitaire to Free Cell, but he was too familiar with that game. It wasn't even a challenge anymore.

He was considering giving Minesweeper a try when Sally came to his door.

"Hey," he said, remembering his original plan. "Want to get some lunch? We could go back to the Tea Room."

The mention of the restaurant jiggled something in Sally's subconscious, something she thought might be important, but she couldn't quite say what it was. She tried to focus on it, but nothing came clear.

"I don't usually eat lunch," she said. "I wanted you to go somewhere with me."

"Where?"

"To Ellen Baldree's house. I'm worried about her."

"You don't need to worry about her.

She's not going to get your job, no matter how much she wants it."

"I'm not worried about my job. I'm worried about Ellen personally. She didn't come to school today, and she didn't let anybody know she wasn't going to be here."

"That's not like her," Jack said.

"I know, and that's why I want to go check on her. But I didn't want to go alone."

So this was Jack's big chance at redemption. He was going to get to be Sally's bodyguard against the fierce Ellen Baldree. Somehow he didn't think Vera would be impressed.

"You don't need protection," he said, hoping Sally would contradict him. "Sure, Ellen's mean, but she's sneaky mean. She wouldn't attack you or anything."

"I think I'm just now finding out how sneaky she can be," Sally said. "I think she's the one who sent that e-mail about my supposed kinship with Sarah Good. That's why I want you to go with me. I don't want your burly body as protection. I want a witness if she confesses."

Jack couldn't help but be a little disappointed.

"Can I at least give her the third degree?"

"Jack, you don't have to prove yourself to me. You did that a long time ago."

That made Jack feel a little better. He said, "Why do you think Ellen sent the e-mail?"

"I'd rather tell you on the way to her house, if that's all right with you."

"Sure," Jack said, pushing his disappointment aside. "What are we waiting for?"

As they left the building, Jack tried to steer Sally by the classroom where Vera was teaching. He wanted Vera to see them leaving together so he could tell her later how brave he'd been to take on the bodyguarding job. He even felt a faint hope that Vera would feel just the slightest twinge of jealousy if she saw him and Sally leaving the building together.

But Sally wouldn't cooperate. She grabbed Jack's arm and pulled him in the direction of one of the back doors.

"This way is closer to my car," she said, so Jack gave up on his feeble plans and followed her.

"Maybe we could eat lunch later," he said. "If you don't like the Tea Room, we could go somewhere else."

This time, the restaurant's name jarred something loose in Sally's subconscious. The Garden Gnome had been a witch. Maybe that was what she'd tried to focus on earlier. And he hadn't been a Wiccan, but the wicked kind of witch, like Margaret Hamilton in *The Wizard of Oz*. "Oh, I'll get you, and your little dog, too." It sounded silly, but Vera hadn't thought it was silly. Sally was sorry she hadn't mentioned it to Weems, but she'd had too many other things on her mind last night. Besides, Weems would probably just have laughed at her.

"If we don't have any trouble at Ellen's, we can go eat," Sally said. "The Tea Room is fine."

She thought that if she went there again, something else might occur to her. She wasn't sure that the bit about Curtin and witchcraft was what she really needed to remember.

"Sounds good," Jack said, hoping that by some quirk of fate Vera would stop by and see him and Sally there.

Then she'll be sorry, he thought.

From Cotton Mather's Memorable Providences Relating to Witchcraft and Possession

Go tell Mankind, that there are Devils and Witches; and that though those night-birds least appear where the daylight of the Gospel comes, yet New England has had examples of their existence and operation; and that not only the Wigwams of Indians, where the pagan pow-wows often raise their masters, in the shapes of bears and snakes and fires, but the house of Christians, where our God has had his constant worship, have undergone the annoyance of evil spirits. Go tell the world, What prays can do beyond all devils and witches, and what it is that these monsters love to do; and though the demons in the audience of several standers-by threatened much disgrace to thy author, if he let thee come abroad, yet venture that, and in this way seek a just revenge on them for the disturbance they have given to such as have called on the name of god.

21

Ellen lived in an old house in the part of town that had been built by some of its earliest settlers. The house was nearly a hundred years old. It was a rambling wooden structure with big windows on all sides. The house had been designed for the days before air-conditioning, when it was important to let even the slightest breeze waft through the rooms to cool them, if you could call that cooling. The windows were all closed now because Ellen had put in central heat and air when she bought the place several years earlier.

The house had only one story, but there was a large attic, and it too had windows, though only on two sides. Sally didn't know whether Ellen had finished out the attic, which was what Sally would have done if she'd owned the place. She would have loved to have the space for an office/library.

The yard was one of those Chamber of Commerce yard-of-the-month contenders.

Sally didn't particularly like to work in the yard, but she admired people who did. Ellen's grass was perfectly trimmed. The sidewalk and driveway were edged. There was no grass growing in the flower beds that ran along the front of the house, just gardenia and azalea bushes that grew in the well-mulched soil surrounded by periwinkles.

"I wish she'd come over and do my yard," Jack said.

"I don't think she'd be willing to do mine even if I paid her," Sally said as she drove her Acura into the short driveway.

When the house had been built, there hadn't been much use for a driveway, and the garage was just a small building that might have been added to the property to house a Model T, though it would have been a tight fit.

Jack got out of Sally's car and tried to see inside the garage. But the door was made of wood, and there were no windows in the building.

"She could be out of town," Jack said when Sally joined him.

"Why would she leave town?"

"Maybe she found out you were onto her."

"She couldn't possibly have known, and

even if she did, what good would leaving town do her? She'd have to come back sooner or later. Let's knock on the door."

Sally went to the front of the house. A porch ran along the entire front and around to the side. A high-backed wooden rocker sat near the front door, and a wooden swing hung from the ceiling. There was no doorbell, so Sally hammered on the screen door with the heel of her hand. The door was loose in the frame and it jumped around, making quite a bit of noise as she pounded on it, but no one answered.

Sally looked around for Jack. He was still over at the garage, trying to pull back the door.

"Jack," Sally said. "Come over here."

He let go of the door and said, "There's a car in there. I could see it. I don't know if it's Ellen's."

Sally didn't know whose else it could be. She banged on the door again. Still no one came or called.

"I'm going to try the back," Sally told Jack.

She came off the porch and followed a flagstone walk around to the back of the house. Jack went with her.

Ellen's back yard was even more impressive than the front. There was a clump of banana trees, a big oak for shade, some bamboo, and even a little fishpond. A wooden bench rested under the oak near its trunk.

"This is really nice," Jack said, looking around.

Sally wasn't interested in the yard. She wanted to find Ellen. She walked up a couple of concrete steps to the screened-in porch and knocked on the screen door.

"Ellen! Are you in there?"

"Did it ever occur to you that she might be hiding?" Jack said. "If she did send that e-mail, you're the last person she'd want to see."

He was right. Sally said, "You call her, then."

"Me?"

"You. Come on up here."

Jack stepped up beside Sally and called Ellen's name, but he got no more response than she had.

"She's not here," Jack said. "Or she's hiding out. Either way, we're wasting our time."

Sally pulled the screen door open.

"Oh, no," Jack said. "I'm not going in there. That's illegal."

"It's not illegal if the door's open," Sally

said, though she was pretty sure that wasn't true. "And nobody asked you to go in."

"Well, I'm not. If this were a movie, we'd go in there and Ellen would be dead on the floor with a knife sticking out of her back."

Sally went through the door and stood on the porch. A white wicker table and chairs sat to one side. Hanging baskets that held spider plants dangled from the ceiling. It was a pleasant place, but too warm.

Across from Sally there was another door, this one leading into the house, probably into the kitchen. Sally took three steps across the wooden floor and took hold of the handle.

"I don't think you should go in there," Jack said from behind her. He was standing just inside the screen door.

"I thought you weren't coming in."

"This is as far as I go. I don't think you should open that door. Let's leave."

Sally turned the knob and the door swung inward.

"Ellen? Are you all right?"

"I'm leaving," Jack said. "You're about to get in real trouble."

"Nobody asked you to stay."

Sally went through the door and into the kitchen. The interior of the house was cool, and Sally could hear the central air unit humming away.

The kitchen was neat, as Sally would have expected from everything she'd seen so far. Not as neat as Mae Wilkins's kitchen, maybe, but it would do. No dirty dishes in the sink, the tops of the table and counters all spic and span, the stove top gleaming. The countertops were white granite with flecks of black. A coffeemaker sat on the counter, with an electric can opener and a mixer nearby. The electric stove and side-by-side refrigerator were both white and looked new.

"This is it," Jack said. "I'm not going one step farther."

Sally turned and gave him a look.

"Just go sit in the car and wait for me," she said. "You're starting to get on my nerves."

"I'm just trying to get you to do the right thing. We don't have any business in here."

"I do. One of my faculty members didn't report for work today, and I'm going to find out why. Maybe she's sick and needs help."

"When you put it that way, it doesn't sound so bad. But what if we find her dead body in the living room?"

"We'll look around for Colonel Mustard."

"Very funny," Jack said.

Sally went into the next room, which was the dining room. Three long windows let in the sunlight. An antique sideboard stood against a wall, and in the middle of the room was a Duncan Phyfe table. Sally suspected that it was faux Phyfe.

"Fee, fie, faux Phyfe," she said under her breath.

"What?" Jack said.

"Nothing."

Sally didn't think the six Queen Anne chairs around the dining table were genuine antiques, either. If they were, Ellen was making a lot more money than Sally. Or she'd come into a big inheritance.

There were two exits from the dining room, both leading to hallways. Sally picked one of them and stood in the entrance to the hall.

"Ellen? Are you feeling all right?" she called.

No answer, except from Jack, who said, "We really shouldn't be here. It just doesn't feel right to be roaming around in someone's house when we don't even know if she's home."

"I thought I told you to go wait in the car."

"I didn't want to."

"All right, but keep quiet. Look, there's her home office at the end of the hall."

A light was on in the room. Sally started forward without looking to see if Jack was following. She stopped when she heard a noise from behind her, from the direction of the kitchen. She thought that Jack had left after all, but when she turned to look, Jack was standing right behind her.

"I heard something in the kitchen," she said. "Did someone come in?"

"I hope not," Jack said. "But I heard it, too."

Sally looked past him. She could see part of the dining room and part of the kitchen, but she didn't see anyone in either one of them.

"Maybe it was my imagination."

"I hope so. I don't want anybody to catch us in here. I've been to jail once, and I didn't like it."

"You were there for an hour or two. That doesn't make you a hardened ex-con. You didn't even get a tattoo."

"I didn't trust the needles," Jack said.

Sally didn't reply. She turned back to look down the hall and heard another noise behind her. This time she was sure it had come from the kitchen.

"Somebody's in there," she said.

"Maybe it's Ellen," Jack said.

"Ellen?" Sally said. "Is that you? We were worried about you, and the door was open, so we just came on in."

Someone moved to stand just beyond the doorway between the kitchen and the dining room. Whoever it was, it wasn't Ellen, being taller, wider, and male.

"What the hell are you doing in here?" the newcomer said.

"Uh-oh," Jack said.

Sally was glad he hadn't said *I told you so.*

The man was in shadow, as the light from the windows didn't reach him, and Sally couldn't make out his features.

"I asked what you were doing here," he said.

Sally thought she recognized the voice.

"Larry? Larry Lawrence."

Lawrence came through the doorway and into the dining room.

"That's right, and I'm going to ask you one more time, what are you doing here?"

"We were worried about Ellen," Jack told him. "She didn't show up at the college this morning, and that's not like her. We thought she might be sick."

Sally admired the way he had picked up on her excuse.

"And by the way," he added, "what are *you* doing here?"

Larry swaggered around the table. He was in his middle fifties, but solid as a stump. His hair was still thick and his step springy. He swung his arms like a man looking for a fight.

"I'm the one asking the questions," he said.

Jack didn't back down. He took a step toward Larry.

"That's what you think."

Just what I needed, Sally thought. A macho fest. She reached out and put a hand on Jack's arm.

"Just hold on," she told him.

Jack shook her hand off, but he didn't move any closer to Larry.

Sally said, "Larry, we've told you why we came, and I think we have as much right as you to be here. Or more, since you haven't told us your reason."

"Yeah," Jack said.

"Hush, Jack. Well, Larry?"

"It's not any of your business."

"It might be. But even if you think it's not, think about this: Jack and I aren't moving from this spot until you tell us why you're here, so if Ellen's in trouble, she's not going to get any help."

Larry took a while to think that over, but Sally didn't mind waiting. As long as he and Jack weren't fighting, she was satisfied.

"All right," Larry said after about half a minute. "I don't see what difference it'll make if I tell you. Ellen's working with me on the Citizens for Fiscal Responsibility. I tried to call her a couple of times at the college this morning, times I knew she wasn't in class. I didn't get an answer, so I called Wynona. She said Ellen hadn't showed up today, and I came to check on her."

"Very considerate of you," Jack said, though he didn't sound to Sally as if he meant it. "Too bad Ellen's on the wrong side of the bond issue."

Sally was thinking the same thing. She couldn't understand why a faculty member would want the bond to fail. And then it hit her. For Ellen, secretly opposing the bond was an underhanded way to get revenge on the college administration for its collective failure to recognize her distinguished qualifications and appoint her department chair.

"We've been trying to recruit more faculty members, and even some students," Larry said. "Ellen was helping us. She gave us some names, and we picked up some volunteers after people read our ads in the paper."

"That's a good story," Jack said. "It's too bad I don't believe you."

"Why not?" Sally said.

"If she was just a member of his little conspiracy, he wouldn't be so worried about her. There's bound to be more to it than that."

"I was also worried about her," Larry said, "because she's a . . . friend."

Oh, Sally thought, realizing by the way he said the word *friend* that Jack was right. There was a little more to Larry's relationship with Ellen than he'd implied at first. She'd never thought of Ellen as the type to have a romantic relationship, but then she'd never thought of Larry that way, either. His wife had been dead for several years. Maybe he was lonely. Maybe Ellen was, too.

"Look," Larry said, softening his voice, "I'm sorry I tried to act tough with you, but I'm worried about Ellen. And we're just standing around here doing nothing."

"We were about to look in the office," Sally said. "You can come along."

"I'll check the bedroom," he said, and went into the other hallway.

"He knows where her bedroom is," Jack said.

"We're all grown-ups here, Jack. At least most of the time."

"I didn't mean to act like a jerk. Larry started it."

"Jack, please."

"Sorry. Let's check the office."

The office held a computer desk with a flat-screen Dell monitor on it, a small writing desk, an ergonomic chair that could roll between the two desks on the hardwood floor, and a portable color TV that sat on a low table.

Ellen Baldree was there, too, lying on the floor, legs and arms outstretched, mouth open, eyes closed.

"Damn," Jack said. "She's dead."

22

This time Jack couldn't resist.

"I knew we shouldn't have come in here," he said.

"At least there's no knife in her back," Sally said. "You said there'd be a knife in her back. Of course, she's lying faceup, so it's possible that there's a knife and we just can't see it."

"How can you make jokes about this? We're here in the house illegally, and a dead woman's lying in the middle of the floor. Not only that, the dead woman is our friend."

"Shouldn't you say *was* our friend?"

"Holy Moly," Jack said. "I never knew you were so cold-blooded. The joke was bad enough, but verb tense?"

"Calm down and take a deep breath, Jack."

"I don't need to take a deep breath. And I'm not excited."

"Just humor me."

Jack exhaled, then took a breath.

"Smell it?"

"Yeah, I do. Smells like cheap wine."

"Not so cheap," Sally said, pointing to a bottle on the floor beside the writing desk.

"Oh," Jack said, bending down to look at the label. "Well, it smells like moderately priced wine, then."

At that moment, Larry Lawrence came into the office behind them.

"Ellen!" he said when he saw her. "My God, what have they done to you?"

"Nothing," Sally said. "If you'll look, you'll see that she's breathing, and if you'll listen, you might even hear her snore."

"In other words," Jack said, "she's snockered."

"I don't believe it."

"Believe it," Sally told him, and she pointed out the bottle.

"But that's not like her at all," Larry said, pushing past Sally and Jack to kneel beside Ellen. He lifted her head. "Ellen. Ellen. Wake up."

"It might be a while if she drank that whole bottle of wine this morning," Sally said.

It looked to Sally as if Ellen had been sitting at the writing desk before she passed out, so she went over to see what Ellen had been working on, if someone in her condition could be said to have been working.

A sheet of white paper lay on the desk, and Ellen had been writing on it with a ballpoint pen.

"Should we call nine-one-one?" Jack asked.

"That's for emergencies only," Sally told him. "A drunk woman isn't an emergency. Larry, why don't you take her to her bed. She'd be more comfortable there."

"That's a good idea," Larry said.

When he picked Ellen up, she was limp as linguine. He turned sideways so he could get through the door with her and carried her off down the hall.

"She didn't look uncomfortable to me," Jack said.

"I don't know if she was or not, but I didn't want Larry around while I'm snooping."

"Snooping? What snooping? I don't think snooping is a good idea. We should just leave now."

"Not yet," Sally said.

She took the paper off the desk and tried to read it. At first glance it seemed to be nothing but an incoherent scrawl, but Sally was skilled at reading papers written by freshman students under strict time constraints. She thought she could read just about most people's scrawl, whether they were drunk or sober when they had set it down.

"Here's her glass," Jack said.

It was lying on the floor behind the wine bottle, and Sally saw that a ballpoint pen lay there as well. Jack picked up the glass and bottle and set them on the desk. He didn't bother with the pen.

"What does that note say?" he asked.

"It looks like an apology to me. I think she must have started to drink and to write it at about the same time. The first part is more legible than the rest."

"Guilty conscience," Jack said. "She had to fortify herself to write it. The more she wrote, the more fortification she needed. No wonder she wasn't in class this morning."

"Her first class isn't until nine. She probably started writing this around eight, thinking she'd be finished by time to leave for school."

And she would have, Sally thought, if she'd been able to do it sober.

"She didn't have the nerve to write it," Jack said. "She wanted to write it, but she needed help."

"Write what?" Larry asked, coming back into the office.

"A note to me," Sally said. "She was apologizing for something."

"What?"

"Nothing important," Sally told him. If Larry didn't know about the e-mail, she wasn't going to tell him.

She folded the paper and put it in her purse. She wasn't going to leave it there for Ellen to find and tear up when she was sober again.

"She didn't have anything to apologize for," Larry said. "The college treated her shabbily, and she was helping us bring a sense of fiscal responsibility to the place."

"That's baloney," Jack said. "You both had an ax to grind."

Larry held up his hands, palms outward.

"Not true. We're just civic-minded citizens, doing what we think is best for the town and the school."

"Hoo-boy," Jack said. "Surely you don't expect us to believe that."

"Believe whatever you like. It happens to be the truth."

"If the bond doesn't pass, the college is going to have some financial problems," Sally said. "We need to upgrade all the computers in the faculty offices, buy new classroom furniture, update all the labs, overhaul the air-conditioning and heating system, fix up the library, and do a million other things."

"That's the problem with everyone at the college," Larry said. "Well, not everyone. Ellen saw the light."

"What light would that be?" Jack asked. "The one on the front of the oncoming train?"

"No, the one that illuminates the part of your brain that tells you the students can sit in the old desks for a few more years and that everyone can get by with the old heating and AC system. And that the old computers are just fine for what you use them for. Playing solitaire doesn't require state-of-the-art machines."

"We use computers for research," Jack said. "And word processing. Not games."

Sally thought it was remarkable that he kept a straight face while telling that whopper.

"Who else besides Ellen have you recruited from the faculty?" she asked.

"That's private information."

"I don't believe you've recruited anyone," Jack said. "But I think the Gnome was trying to recruit me."

Larry gave Jack a speculative look. "He

thought you might have caught on to him. But he wasn't trying to recruit you. He was just feeling you out, trying to see if you were interested. He thought you might be one of the first to sign up after Ellen did."

"I don't know what could have given him that idea. He and I were never friends, and I never encouraged him to think I had any differences with the college."

"I think Ellen gave him the idea," Larry said. "She thought that maybe you'd be interested after . . ."

He paused and looked at Sally.

"After what?" she said.

"After you threw him over for Jorge Rodriguez."

Jack was indignant. "Hey, she didn't throw me over. We were never even an item. I've been going out with Vera Vaughn."

"Ellen told us about that, and Harold decided not to call you anymore. He figured all your energy would be directed elsewhere."

"Is that a crack?"

"Just an observation."

"All right," Sally said before they could carry the conversation any further. "That's enough of that. Is Ellen doing all right?"

"I hope so," Larry said. "I still can't believe she got drunk and passed out."

"The evidence is overwhelming," Sally said. "Are you going to stay here for a while and look after her?"

"Yes, I'll do that."

"Then Jack and I should get back to the college. We both have office hours. But before we go, I have one more thing I want to say to you if you'll let me."

"Why do I get the feeling that I couldn't stop you even if I said *no*?"

Jack laughed, but Sally ignored him. She said, "I know that you think Chief Desmond is a rat, but he's sorry for what happened with your daughter, and he's trying to do the right thing. You should concentrate on helping her and forget about this bond issue."

"Desmond can't change what he did, no matter how bad he feels about it now. And I'm not going to change my position. Now that Harold's dead, a lot of people are counting on me to pick up the slack. I'm not going to let them down."

"How long were you at the college?" Jack said. "Twenty-two years? Twenty-three? You made a good living there for all that time, and when you retired, you got a generous settlement. The school's still paying for your health and dental insurance. But you want to stab everybody there in the back because one guy made a mistake. That's pretty dumb if you ask me."

"I didn't ask you," Larry said. "And you don't know what my daughter's been through, so don't tell me what's dumb and what's not. Just go back to the campus and keep your office hours."

Testosterone strikes again, Sally thought.

She touched Jack's sleeve. He looked at her, and she shook her head.

"Sorry," he said, and they both turned and left the house.

23

Sally couldn't concentrate on the papers she was supposed to be grading because she kept thinking about Ellen Baldree. She even felt a little sorry for her.

Ever since her arrival on the HCC campus, Sally had known that Ellen didn't like her. That had become obvious when Sally had taken over as department chair, and it still was. And all the while that Ellen had been pretending to be the model of a cooperative professional, she'd been wondering about how she was going to make Sally suffer for having gotten the job that Ellen craved for her own.

It struck Sally that Ellen wasn't all that much different from the women who had been accused of witchcraft in Salem. She was a woman alone, embittered by her experience and without many friends, even in the English department. In fact, Sally wasn't sure Ellen had any friends at all, which might be another reason she'd signed on with the Citizens for Fiscal Responsibility. She could have been looking for a community to be a part of, a group that would welcome her.

She'd been welcomed, all right, especially by Larry Lawrence, who was as bitter and lonely as Ellen. Or even more bitter.

What bothered Sally most about her speculations was that she herself wasn't really that much different from Ellen when she thought about it. Her situation was in fact about the same.

Except that Sally had friends. Jack was a friend, and so, oddly enough, was Vera Vaughn.

And then there was Lola. Ellen didn't have a cat like Lola, or any cat for that matter, and Sally was sure Ellen's life was the poorer for it.

Sally also had her mother. Maybe Ellen had a mother, but Sally didn't know if that was a benefit to Ellen or not.

Ellen had also found a love life, something Sally had not done since her husband's death. She didn't feel any great loss, not so far. She'd been mildly attracted to Jack, and strongly attracted to Jorge, but when neither of those romances had worked out, Sally hadn't been bothered in the least.

Oh, all right, she admitted to herself that losing Jorge to Mae Wilkins did bother her a little. If she were really a witch, she'd put a spell on Mae's house so that no matter how hard Mae tried, the floors would never be quite clean, the windows never quite sparkling, the rooms never quite tidy.

Sally didn't like the way her speculations were leading her. She'd started feeling sorrier for herself than she felt for Ellen, and that was bad. Self-pity wasn't among her favorite emotions.

She opened her purse and took out the note that Ellen had been writing to have another look at it.

Ellen had felt guilty enough to apologize for the e-mail stunt, but, according to the note, only because Jennifer and Sherm Jackson had told her about the events of the previous evening. It seemed their behavior was too over the top even for Ellen.

But there was more to the note than that. Unfortunately, Sally was having trouble making it out. Not only was it almost illegible, but Ellen had either spilled wine on it or drooled on it, causing the ink to smear. Sally preferred the wine hypothesis, but either way, the paper was impossible to read.

No, not impossible. Sally wasn't going to

give up so easily. She'd taught creative writing for years before the advent of computers and campus computer labs. She'd had students whose handwriting was so small that she had to use a magnifying glass to read it, students who deliberately tried to obscure their spelling errors by scrawling or blurring the words, students whose writing was so naturally bad that it gave chicken-scratching a bad name. And she had read every single one of their papers and commented on every one of them as well. She wasn't going to be defeated by anything that Ellen had written.

Sally wondered if the final portion of Ellen's note said something about the Garden Gnome's death. Was it possible that Ellen had not gotten drunk entirely because of what she'd done to Sally? Was there something else that Ellen felt guilty about and wanted to tell Sally?

Concentrating on the writing, if it could be called that, Sally was almost certain she could make out the word *blood*. The only connection she could make with that word was between it and the way Harold Curtin had died.

And that connection started Sally down a completely different trail. What if the Garden Gnome had committed suicide, leaving behind the notes about "blood to drink" in order to implicate Sally in his death.

Or, to take it in another direction, what if Ellen had killed Curtin herself, after getting him to write the "blood" notes in order to put the blame for his death on Sally.

Either of those scenarios would make a twisted kind of sense to someone like Ellen or the Gnome, but even if they made sense, Sally told herself that it wasn't her job to find out who had killed Curtin. That was Lieutenant Weems's job. The city paid him to do it, and Sally was happy to let him. She had been mixed up in a couple of murders, and she hadn't liked it either time. On the other hand, if Ellen or Curtin wanted to tie her to Curtin's death, Sally wanted to give Weems all the help she could.

She wondered if he had investigated the fact that Jennifer and Sherm Jackson had arrived at Curtin's house almost as soon as the HCC delegation had left on the night of Curtin's death. But it wasn't her job to tell him about that. Surely Desmond had told him by now.

Sally didn't like to think that Jennifer or Sherm or the two of them together would kill someone, and she couldn't think of any reason why they would kill Curtin. But the look in Jennifer's eyes the previous evening was enough to convince Sally that Jennifer might be capable of anything, no matter what Sally might want to think. Still, Sally wasn't a law enforcement officer, so she'd let Weems worry about the Jacksons. He could check their alibis and the evidence, and then he could either eliminate them or implicate them.

She put aside the note Ellen had been writing, telling herself that she would read it later, when she got home.

Right now, she needed to get some student papers graded. She took one off the top of the stack and got started.

Unlike Sally, Jack was feeling chipper. He'd stood up to Larry Lawrence, who outweighed him by a good forty pounds. So what if Larry was a few years older? He was bigger and probably stronger than Jack and the way Jack saw it, Larry was the one pushing for a fight.

He knew Sally didn't see it quite the same way, and he'd even apologized for acting like a jerk.

But his apology hadn't been sincere. If there had been a jerk in the room, it had been Larry. Larry had forced him to take a stand, and he'd done it. Several times. He wished Vera had been there to see him. He was sure she would have thought him courageous instead of foolish.

He wondered if he would have acted differently with Larry if instead of calling the police last night, he'd gone out onto the lawn and joined in the fray. He didn't think so. Calling the cops was the right thing to do, and it had kept anyone from getting hurt.

The call had also irritated Weems, and Jack considered that a very good thing indeed. He had to give Weems credit, however, for coming right out. He hadn't even objected when Jack had told him the reason for his call.

One thing that still rankled Jack was that the Garden Gnome had actually thought Jack would be a good candidate for the Citizens for Fiscal Responsibility because Sally had dumped him.

As Jack had told Larry, nobody had dumped anybody, unless of course Vera had dumped Jack because of the call. Jack hadn't mentioned that possibility to Larry.

Maybe he should have clobbered Larry when he made that crack about Jack's energy. And it was a crack, no matter what

Larry said. However, since Jack, if pressed, would have been forced to admit that Larry had a point, there was no need to push things or to say any more about it. Vera was certainly demanding, not that Jack minded. He was enjoying his new relationship, and he hoped it wasn't over.

And it wasn't. Shortly before three o'clock, Vera came by Jack's office. He was doing a little research, trying to verify something that he'd heard or read years before about George Jones and the Big Bopper singing the "oom-bah oom-bah" backup on Johnny Preston's recording of "Running Bear."

"How would you like to take me somewhere and make up?" Vera said.

She looked quite provocative to Jack, but then she nearly always looked quite provocative to him.

"Sure," he said, proud that his voice didn't quaver. "Your place or mine."

"You're the boss," Vera said, without a trace of irony as far as Jack could tell.

Jack started to put his books and papers away.

"Yours," he said.

24

When Sally got home around four, Lola was frisking around the house, so Sally gave her a kitty treat and got out the old piece of rope that Lola liked to attack.

Sally dragged the rope along the rug, and Lola crouched down as close to the floor as she could get, her feet stretched in front of her, her tail switching from side to side.

When the end of the rope was about to disappear around the end of the couch, Lola charged.

For a cat of her weight and bulk, Lola was surprisingly quick and nimble. She covered a distance of seven or eight feet before Sally could twitch the end of the rope out of her reach.

She grabbed the rope between her paws and got it into her mouth in one smooth motion, rolling on her back and scratching at the rest of the rope with her back paws at the same time.

"If you were an outside cat," Sally said,

"you'd clear the neighborhood of birds in no time."

Lola rolled to a sitting position and said, "Meow."

"I know. And that's one reason why you're not an outside cat. We don't want to decimate the bird population. The members of the Audubon Society wouldn't approve."

"Meow," Lola said.

"Yes, I know you don't care about the Audubon Society, but birds are our friends."

"Meow."

"Are you being sarcastic?"

"Meow."

"Well, stop it."

I'm really losing it, Sally thought as she went to check Lola's food and water. I'm having a conversation with a cat. I need to get out more. Maybe it was a mistake to let Mae get her hooks into Jorge so easily.

Lola followed along after Sally as if to make sure the job was done right. Sally got the water bowl, washed it out, and put in fresh water. She had two faucets on the sink, one for washing and one with a filter for drinking water. She used the filtered water for Lola, who was winding herself around Sally's ankles.

"I hope you appreciated the special treatment," Sally said.

"Meow."

"Good. Now come drink some of the nice fresh water."

Sally put the bowl back and Lola dutifully drank from it. Sally wasn't sure if Lola was thirsty or if she was drinking just to mollify Sally. After she finished lapping up the water, Lola went into the bedroom. After all the strenuous activity, she needed a nap.

Because she'd skipped lunch, Sally thought she'd treat herself to something special for dinner, which meant a hamburger, followed by a Klondike Heath Bar Crunch. Keeping the Klondike bars in the house was a severe temptation, but Sally was able to resist them for the most part. She ate them only when she cooked a hamburger for herself, and she didn't cook hamburgers often. She didn't cook anything often.

She checked first to be sure that she had an onion in the refrigerator. As far as she was concerned, hamburger without onion was no hamburger at all, and she was happy to see that she had half a 1015 onion in the vegetable drawer.

She heated her big iron skillet on the

stove and when it was ready, she put a frozen meat patty in it. The sound of the sizzle brought Lola back to the kitchen.

"I thought you were taking a nap," Sally said.

Lola didn't answer. She sat near the stove, looking up at Sally.

"You're not getting a hamburger," Sally told her. "Go on back to sleep."

Lola gave her a low-level hiss and left the kitchen. Sally hissed back at Lola's retreating tail, then opened the pantry and got out the potato chips, feeling virtuous that they were baked, not fried. She wasn't having French fries, and the hamburger patty was made from extra-lean beef. Why, she was preparing what amounted to a low-fat meal. That is, if she didn't count the Klondike bar, which she wasn't.

When the patty was done, Sally scooped it out of the pan with a spatula and put it on a paper towel to drain. She turned off the heat and put a bun in the pan to let it warm in the little bit of grease that was left behind. She flattened it with the spatula. Then she sliced the onion. No one was coming by, as far as she knew, so she cut a generous slice. There was a tomato in the refrigerator, too, so she cut a slice of that as well. She put the bun on a plate, spread

264

some mustard on it, and put the patty on top of that. Then she added the onion, the tomato, some pickles, and some lettuce. She poured herself a glass of Diet Pepsi to go with it.

Chips, an old-fashioned hamburger, Diet Pepsi, and an ice cream bar afterward. Life was good.

She was getting the Klondike bar from the freezer when she thought about the note from Ellen Baldree. Maybe reading it with ice cream in hand would help.

It didn't. There were still parts of it that were simply impossible to read, no matter how much skill Sally had developed in her years of grading papers.

Sally decided she was going to have to do what she hadn't even wanted to consider. She was going to have to call Ellen.

She could go by and see how Ellen was doing, but she didn't like that idea at all. She thought that Larry Lawrence might still be there. She didn't want to talk to Larry again.

She was sure that Ellen, if she was awake, wasn't going to be feeling well, anyway, but maybe she could function well enough to discuss the note. Sally just hoped she could remember having written it.

Larry answered the phone.

I should have known, Sally thought. She asked how Ellen was, and Larry said she was feeling about as well as could be expected.

"Has she eaten anything?"

"I fixed some soup," Larry said, revealing a nurturing side that Sally hadn't suspected.

"I was hoping I could talk to her."

"I don't think she wants to talk to you," Larry said.

Sally could hear Ellen in the background. She was telling Larry something, but Sally couldn't make it out.

"Just a second," Larry said, and he must have covered the receiver with his hand as Sally couldn't hear anything for a while.

When she did hear something again, it was Ellen's voice.

"Sally, are you still there?"

"I'm here. How are you feeling?"

"Not good. My head must be the size of a basketball. I'm sorry I let my classes down today. I promise you that won't happen again."

Sally found herself feeling sorry for Ellen. The e-mail had been a malicious trick, but Sally was sure that Ellen regretted having played it.

"Don't worry about your classes," she said. "They don't have to know why you weren't there. Do you feel like talking about that note you were writing me?"

"You found the note?"

"Yes. I took it with me when I left."

"Larry didn't mention that," Ellen said.

There was silence for a few seconds, and once again Sally had the impression that the receiver was covered.

"Sally?" Ellen said.

"Yes."

"I'm not sure I like it that you took the note. I don't know that I'd have sent it to you."

"The part I can read didn't come as a surprise. I'd already figured out you sent the e-mail. You were seen in my office several times."

"I did it to hurt you. It seems stupid now, and I wish I'd used better judgment."

Sally thought that Ellen was having a hard time saying she was sorry. Maybe she couldn't say it, and that's why writing the note had been so difficult for her.

"You don't have to apologize," she said. "I'm not going to hold the e-mail incident against you. All I want you to do is write another e-mail to everyone you sent the first one to and explain that the first one was a hoax. Will you do that?"

After a pause Ellen said she might be able to bring herself to do that.

"Good," Sally said. "Now let's get back to that note you were writing to me."

"I don't think I want to talk about it."

Sally pretended that she hadn't heard. "The part about blood. I'm not sure what you were trying to say."

"I'm not sure either. Did I mention blood?"

"You know you did." Sally barely kept the exasperation out of her voice. "I'm almost certain that Harold Curtin's name was there, too."

More silence. This time it went on for a while.

"Sally?"

"I'm still here."

"You shouldn't have taken that note. Larry should have stopped you."

"But he didn't. And it had my name on it, after all. I had a perfect right to take it. Now tell me what you were trying to say."

"I don't think I will."

This time it was Sally's turn to be quiet. She wasn't consulting with anyone. She was just considering her options. When she'd made up her mind, she said, "All right. Here's the deal. I might be able to read the letter without your help. If I can, that's fine. If I can't, I'm turning it over to Lieutenant Weems of the Hughes Police Department, just in case it has something to do with Curtin's murder. I have a feeling that if he can't read it, he'll find someone who can."

Ellen was shocked. "You wouldn't do that!"

"I've been your supervisor for a few years now. I think you know that I would."

"You shouldn't be my supervisor," Ellen said. "I should have had that job."

"But you don't have it. I do. Get over it, Ellen. And tell me what you wanted to say in that note."

"I should never have started writing it in the first place. If Harold hadn't died, I wouldn't have."

"Maybe the note does implicate you in his death. I suppose I'll have to hand it over to the police."

"Damn you," Ellen said. "You're black-mailing me."

"No, I'm not. I'm just trying to get you to do the right thing. So tell me what you wrote."

Ellen whined and carried on for another full minute, saying that she had nothing at all to do with Harold Curtin's death; that the note was her personal property, stolen by Sally; that Sally was a cruel and conniving blackmailer; and that Sally might not be a witch, but change the *w* to a *b* and the description in the e-mail was perfectly accurate.

Sally listened to it all and then said, "Fine. Now I've heard you out, and I'm tired of listening. Tell me what was in the note, or I'm hanging up and calling Weems."

So Ellen told her.

From Cotton Mather's
The Wonders of the Invisible World

The witches do say, that they form themselves much after the manner of congregational churches; and that they have a baptism and a supper, and officers among them, abominably resembling those of our Lord.

25

Seepy Benton didn't have a cat. He had four. They had turned up one day in his garage, just kittens at the time, and they seemed to like the place. They had adopted Seepy within minutes, and he was happy that they'd come to live with him. But since they were all black and all looked alike, he could hardly tell them apart.

Each cat had a name: Emily, Leon Trotsky, Sam, and Ralph. The trouble was that he didn't know when he was talking to one or the other of them, except for Emily, who, being female, had not only a slightly different look but a distinctly different personality from the others.

As far as Seepy was concerned, the cats were wonderful, most of the time. But there was a problem: they hated his singing. It was bad enough that no one would listen to his songs at the college, except for Molly, and she listened only because she couldn't escape gracefully. But he found it pretty insulting that even his own cats wouldn't listen. All he had to do was start to tune the guitar, and they would run out of the room and hide somewhere they hoped that he couldn't find them.

Seepy's house contained plenty of places to hide, as he wasn't the best of house-keepers. In fact, when it came to keeping house, he was the anti–Mae Wilkins.

Dusting? Couldn't be bothered.

Newspapers and magazines? Let them accumulate.

Books? Stack them wherever there was a place.

Dishes? Wash them when there were no more clean ones or when the stack in the sink got so high that it was likely to fall over and cause damage.

Clothes? Hang 'em on a chair or whatever was handy.

The clutter didn't bother Seepy in the least. In fact, he hardly noticed it. He was too busy writing songs, working on his Web page, meditating in his flotation tank, taking photographs of fractals on his computer, studying the Talmud or Kabbalah, or working out an astrological chart.

What he was not busy with was his love life, mainly because at the moment he didn't have one. He knew that it was his own fault. He was so absorbed in his many interests that he didn't have time to think about a love life. And, to tell the truth, until recently there wasn't really anyone at the college who'd interested him, except Vera Vaughn, and she had always seemed somewhat intimidating to Seepy, who'd been more than a little surprised when she and Jack Neville got together. Jack had never struck Seepy as being manly enough for someone like Vera, certainly no more manly than C. P. Benton, Ph.D. If they had Olympic competition for sexual athletes, Seepy Benton would be a contender every four years. Well, that might be a slight exaggeration, but still, Jack must have hidden depths that could be plumbed only by someone like Vera.

Lately, however, Seepy had found himself thinking more and more about Sally Good. She was tough but not intimidating, and she had a wry sense of humor. Seepy was sure that anyone he got involved with would need a sense of humor.

Not to mention an ear for music. Seepy sat in a chair in his kitchen and plucked the strings of his guitar, trying to find a tune to go with his latest composition, which he had entitled "Gandhi Wore a Loincloth."

The cats had all disappeared, but he

thought he'd seen one peeking out from behind a stack of newspapers.

Seepy wasn't having much luck with the tune, so he put the guitar aside, standing it in another of the chairs at the table, and got up to see if he had anything to eat.

The inside of his refrigerator depressed him, as there seemed to be a mossy surface on the cheese and an even more interesting growth on top of a bowl of something or other. He couldn't recall what had been in the bowl to begin with, as it had been there for a while. Now, whatever it had once been, it had been transformed into something else entirely. And he didn't think he wanted to eat it.

"Pizza again," he said aloud and went to the telephone to place his order. It would be a vegetarian pizza, naturally, as Seepy had entered a vegetarian phase about a month earlier. Not vegan, so he could have plenty of cheese.

While he was waiting for the pizza to arrive, Seepy thought some more about Sally Good. He wondered what she would think if he dropped by her house. He could play a song or two for her, even though she hadn't expressed an interest in hearing him play when she came by his office. Probably she'd been in a hurry then, and in a more leisurely setting she'd enjoy a tune crafted by a budding songsmith.

He was still thinking it over when the pizza arrived.

Sally wished she hadn't already eaten the Klondike bar. Chocolate would have helped her deal with what Ellen had told her.

It seemed that Ellen knew that Harold had become a witch, and that's what she'd been trying to write about in the illegible part of her note.

Except that Curtin hadn't really joined the coven. He had attended a few of their meetings, which had been disappointingly bland, according to Ellen.

"He was expecting a Black Mass," she told Sally. "Something really satanic, with black robes and hoods, a stone altar with blood in the baptismal font. You know, something right out of 'Young Goodman Brown.' "

Leave it to someone who taught American literature to associate a witches' sabbath with Hawthorne, Sally thought, trying to imagine Curtin in the dream-haunted forest of Hawthorne's mind. It wasn't easy to picture, but she supposed there was a place in there for a garden gnome.

"What he found was a bunch of people who drove BMWs and wore expensive running shoes," Ellen continued.

Sally had a hard time picturing Curtin in a Beemer or even in running shoes. He'd have been more out of place in either than he would have in Hawthorne's dark woods.

"But why did he join a coven in the first place?" she asked.

"It was part of his plan to get back at you for getting him fired."

"He got himself fired. I had nothing to do with it."

"Not to hear him tell it." Ellen's tone was skeptical. "Anyway, it was Harold's idea for me to send the e-mail. He made the connection with your last name and the name of a real-life witch. He said the witch was your ancestor, and he decided he needed to know a little more about witches. He learned all he cared to after about three meetings of the coven. Eventually there would have been more e-mails about you, using some of the information he'd gathered."

Sally thought that Curtin had been using Ellen to do his dirty work, and she thought Ellen was a jerk for going along with him. But she didn't say so.

"What about those references to blood in the note?" Sally said.

"That was from *The House of the Seven Gables*. It had something to do with the witch with your name."

Sally didn't bother to correct her about the name. She said, "Why did that interest him?"

"He thought he could cause you some trouble because of the connection to your ancestor."

"She wasn't my ancestor," Sally said, unable to resist this time.

"Whatever you say. Harold thought differently. Do you want to hear this or not?"

"Go on," Sally said.

"Fine. Harold was fascinated that your ancestor killed someone with a curse. Harold said you'd killed him the same way."

"He was alive at the time."

"He said he might as well have been dead. You took his job away, and then you must have put a curse on the NASDAQ to finish him off."

Would that I had the power, Sally thought, thinking that it would be nice to turn Ellen into a lizard. Or maybe a snail.

"You didn't believe any of that, did you?" she said.

"What I believe or don't believe doesn't matter. Harold believed it. And look what happened to him."

"I had nothing to do with that."

"That's what I'd say if I were you, too."

Sally had taken about all Ellen's guff she could stand, and she thought she had learned just about everything from the note. So she said, "Ellen, I know you don't like me, and I have a feeling you never will. But I'm the department chair, and you're not." Sally hated to steal from Chevy Chase, but it was too good a line to pass up. "You might outlast me, but I don't plan to leave the department anytime soon. In fact, I plan to be at your retirement party to celebrate *your* leaving. If you don't like that idea, then maybe it's time for you to find another place to teach."

"You can't scare me away," Ellen said, but her voice wavered a bit.

"I'm not trying to scare you. I'm just stating the facts."

"Good. Because I'm not scared. I'll be there to teach my classes in the morning."

"See that you are," Sally said, and hung up the phone.

The call hadn't made her feel any better, and now that she'd had a little time to think it over, she thought she could have handled things better. She'd let Ellen get under her skin, and she was sorry about that.

Still, she'd found out what she wanted to know, or she had if Ellen had been telling the truth about the note. Harold Curtin had actually gone to witch meetings to find out ways to torment Sally. If that didn't prove he was crazy, nothing would.

But it didn't help very much with finding out who'd killed him. It was just another piece of a puzzle that still needed a lot of assembly before it looked like anything recognizable.

As far as Sally was concerned, putting the rest of the pieces in their proper places was a job for Lieutenant Weems.

As for Sally, she was going to read a good book.

One without witches.

26

Sally's secret vice, not counting the Hershey bars, was reading what she considered trashy fiction.

Earlier in her career, she had thought that as an English teacher, she should spend her leisure time reading great works of literature. Something by Henry James, perhaps, or Herman Melville.

But in graduate school she had read quite a few of James's novels. She'd read several of them, including *The Wings of the Dove*, more than once. She had even read *The Ambassadors* twice. She thought that was enough.

She loved *Moby Dick*, and she had taken a course in Melville. While reading novels like *Mardi* and *The Confidence Man*, she'd been impressed with Melville's intellect but not his storytelling. So while she'd re-read *Moby Dick* several times, she hadn't read any other Melville since her college days.

What she'd discovered was that she

needed something to relax her, and trashy books seemed to work. She was more likely to read *Peyton Place* than *War and Peace*, more likely to read something by Olivia Goldsmith than anything by Proust.

Tonight she was reading a historical novel by Frank Yerby that she'd found in a used-book store. She didn't think anybody read Yerby anymore, but he'd sold a lot of books in his time, and she was enjoying the book, in spite of Lola, who was being annoying.

Whenever Sally read, Lola would climb in her lap, trying to distract her, and when she succeeded in doing that, she would squirm around, demanding attention.

Sally didn't mind giving the attention, but she also wanted to read, so the attention never lasted long enough to suit Lola, who would then climb up on the back of the chair or couch where Sally was reading and paw at Sally's hair or try to get on her shoulder.

Now she was draped over the back of the chair, attempting to work her way onto a shoulder, when the doorbell rang.

Lola hated the doorbell. Its ring announced that someone was arriving, and Lola didn't like strangers. For that matter she didn't like people with whom she was familiar. She didn't like anyone at all, except Sally. And Sally wasn't sure even that was true all the time.

So before the sound of the bell had died away, Lola was gone. Anyone witnessing her departure might have thought that she was indeed a witch's familiar, as she didn't so much depart as vanish into thin air. One second she was there, and the next she was gone, almost as if she were some kind of digital special effect. Sally knew that she would be under the bed, sulking until whoever was at the door had gone away.

Sally didn't particularly want to be disturbed, but she went to the door and looked through the peephole. It was dark, and the porch light wasn't on, but she could make out Jennifer and Sherm Jackson standing there.

They were about the last people she would have expected to see, given the events of the previous evening. Wondering what they could possibly want, Sally opened the door, without taking off the safety chain. She didn't want to get whacked by an anti-witchcraft sign.

"Can I help you?" she said, speaking through the crack between the door and the frame.

Jennifer Jackson stood in front of her

husband. Her eyes were not as bright as they had been the previous evening, and her hair was lank and stringy as if it hadn't been washed lately. And Sally was sure it hadn't.

"We have to talk to you," Jennifer said in a low, dull voice.

Sally didn't want to talk to Jennifer or to Sherm or to the both of them together. She had nothing to say to either of them.

"It's important," Jennifer said when Sally hesitated. "Can we come in?"

Sally thought that nobody knew the difference between *can* and *may* these days. And what's more, nobody cared, if you didn't count a few old-fogy English teachers. And everyone knew they didn't count.

"It's really important for us to talk to you," Jennifer said. "Please."

Sally could never resist a sincere plea. Sally didn't see any signs, and there was no one else standing outside to take part in some kind of evil home invasion. So even though Jennifer's words didn't sound entirely heartfelt, Sally said, "Just a second" and closed the door to take off the chain.

When she opened the door again, Jennifer grabbed the edge with both hands and slammed it back into Sally's face.

The door smashed into Sally's forehead

with a wood-solid smack and knocked Sally backward. She was stunned and couldn't do a thing do stop Jennifer and Sherm from shouldering their way into the house.

"Close the door, Sherm," Jennifer said. "Lock it. Then close the shutters."

Sherm did as he was told. Sally could see that he was holding something in his hand, but her eyes were watering and her vision was blurry, so she couldn't make out what it was.

She could see what Jennifer was holding all too well, however: a very large knife with a long silvery blade that was pointed right at Sally's midsection.

Sally's head was throbbing, and she could feel a knot starting to form right in the middle of her forehead. She was sure that Jennifer didn't care at all about the knot except to be pleased about having caused it.

"I want you and Sherm to get out right now," Sally said. Her voice was a little unsteady, but not because she was afraid. She was still a little shaken by the blow on the head. "If you leave now, I promise I won't file charges."

Jennifer jabbed at her with the knife, and Sally stepped back a couple of paces.

Jennifer said, "We know what your promises are worth, witch. And we're not worried about you filing any charges. Turn around and go into the living room."

"I'm not going anywhere."

"Oh, yes, you are."

Jennifer jabbed at her with the knife again. Sally thought that she might be able to grab it, but if she did, her hands would be badly cut. She wasn't quite that desperate yet.

"Turn around," Jennifer repeated.

Sally turned, thinking that she could make a break for the bedroom, where the Ladysmith was in the closet. She wished that she hadn't been so safety conscious that she'd made sure the cartridges weren't with the pistol.

But it wouldn't have mattered. Almost as soon as she turned, Sherm's arm snaked around her neck. He jerked it tight, cutting of Sally's air supply.

"Give me the tape," Jennifer said.

Sally heard something hit the floor, maybe the tape. There was silence as Sally tried to breathe, and then she heard a tearing noise.

Sherm moved a little to the side, and Jennifer pulled Sally's arms behind her, putting the wrists together and wrapping them with duct tape.

Sally struggled as hard as she could, but

there wasn't much she could do against Sherm. Every movement she made just took a little more of what air she had left in her lungs. Not enough was left to make a struggle worthwhile.

A hand grabbed Sally's ankle, and Sally kicked backward. Her foot connected with something, but not hard enough to do much damage.

Jennifer didn't like it, however.

"Witch!" she said.

She dropped down to the floor, forced Sally's feet together, and whipped the duct tape around the ankles.

"Drag her to a chair," Jennifer said, and Sherm complied, dragging Sally along as if she were a sack of potatoes.

He didn't put her in a chair. He dropped her on the couch. Sally fell on her side and rolled to the floor, taking in deep gulps of air. Her head, already throbbing, thunked the coffee table.

"I said *chair*, you idiot," Jennifer told Sherm.

Sherm slid his hands under Sally's armpits and lifted her into a chair with arms on both sides. She started to slither to the floor, but Jennifer was there with the knife. She pressed the point up under Sally's chin.

"No you don't," she said.

Sally didn't, and Jennifer removed the knife.

Sally said, "You're crazy."

"Not in the least," Jennifer said. "You're the crazy one. You're a witch."

"That's not true. You're just stupid if you believe that."

Jennifer smiled. "*I'm* stupid? I'm not the one sitting there with duct tape on my wrists and ankles, am I? I guess we know who's stupid, don't we, Sherm."

Sherm nodded.

Jennifer turned grim again. "You've really caused a lot of trouble, you know that, witch?"

Sally's head hurt, and she had no idea what Jennifer was talking about.

"I'm not a witch, and I haven't caused you any trouble."

"You think being hauled off to jail and questioned isn't trouble? You think having your reputation in the community destroyed isn't trouble?"

Sally was catching on now. She said, "I'm not the one who told the police you were at Harold Curtin's apartment the night he was killed."

"Ha. If you weren't, how did you know we were there? How did you know someone even told the police?"

Sally just shook her head. She didn't feel like explaining, and she knew Jennifer wouldn't believe her if she tried.

"I'm sorry it happened. I was questioned by the police, too, so I know what it's like. Now let me go and get out of my house."

"Oh, you're not going to get out of it that easy," Jennifer said.

Easily, Sally thought. "I've said I was sorry. What else do you want to do to me? You've already committed at least two felonies since you got here."

"You're going to suffer for your crimes," Jennifer said, brandishing the knife. "Do you know what that means?"

"That you're going to keep on talking?"

Jennifer gave Sally an odd look.

"Do you think this is funny?" she asked.

"Not in the least."

"Well, good. Because it's not. You are *reprobate*. Do you know what that means?"

"I've never heard the word used that way before, so I'm afraid not. But I'm sure you're going to tell me."

"Yes, I am. It means that you're foreordained to damnation."

"Now you're the one who's being funny."

Jennifer handed Sherm the knife. He took it and let his hand drop to his side.

Jennifer stepped up to Sally and slapped her face.

Sally's head snapped to the side. She felt her face sting and grow warm where Jennifer's hand struck her.

"That's another felony," she said.

"And that's not the end of it," Jennifer said. "Do you know the Bible?"

"I know what it is, if that's what you mean."

"That's not what I mean at all. To know the Bible means that you're familiar with the scriptures. Are you familiar with them?"

"Some of them," Sally said. " 'Do unto others as you would have them do unto you' is one I remember."

Jennifer's grim look turned pious.

"The Devil can quote scripture to his purpose, and you're in league with the Devil for certain and sure."

"I suppose you had another scripture in mind."

"Yes, we did. Didn't we, Sherm?"

Sally thought that Sherm might actually say something that time, but he didn't. He just nodded. He had a vacant look, as if he were thinking about something else, such as how to calculate the quarterly payments on an auto insurance policy with comprehensive coverage and a hundred-dollar deductible.

"We were thinking of Exodus twenty-two, eighteen," Jennifer said. "Do you know that one?"

"Not off the top of my head."

" 'Thou shalt not suffer a witch to live.' I'm sure you've heard it."

For the first time since Jennifer and Sherm had burst into her house, Sally felt a twinge of fear.

The knife hadn't scared her at first because she didn't think Jennifer would kill her with it, but looking at it now, dangling from the golem-like Sherm's hand, Sally changed her mind. Jennifer could kill her. Or Sherm would do it if Jennifer asked him to do it.

Jennifer followed Sally's gaze. She smiled a thin smile.

"You don't have to worry about the knife. We're not going to use a knife. That's not how witches are killed."

Sally had a terrible feeling that she knew what Jennifer had in mind, but she had to ask.

"How do you plan to do it, then?"

"You should know. It happened to your ancestor, and it's going to happen to you."

"Sarah Good wasn't my ancestor," Sally

said. She was getting tired of making the same explanation again and again. "She was my husband's ancestor, so I'm not related to her by blood. And she was no more a witch than I am."

"She was condemned to death, and they hung her."

"Hanged," Sally said.

Jennifer slapped her again.

"I always hated it when English teachers corrected me in school. I don't like it any better now. And it doesn't matter what word I use because the end result is going to be the same."

Sally thought about telling her that *end result* was redundant. But she didn't think getting slapped again would be worth it.

Jennifer smiled at her. It was a horrible smile.

"Go get the rope, Sherm," she said.

27

Seepy Benton put aside his Hebrew lesson.

At one time he had embraced his Native American heritage, identifying with his Indian ancestors, studying their ways, and learning a great deal about them and himself in the process. He had long benefited from meditation, and he had gone so far as to build an authentic sweat lodge in his back yard.

But after a few years, he still felt that there was something lacking in his life. That was when he had begun to explore the Jewish side of his heritage. He had discovered an instant connection with Jewish beliefs, and he was almost willing to accept the idea that the Native Americans were the Lost Tribe of Israel.

He soon found himself entering fully into the Jewish faith, and he was learning Hebrew so that he could read Torah in the original language. He planned eventually to learn Aramaic, as well, but that was a project that might well be years in the future.

As interested as he was in learning the language of his ancestors, or some of his ancestors, he couldn't concentrate. He kept thinking of Sally Good and wondering if she might not like to hear one or two of his musical compositions.

Even if she wouldn't, she might not mind if he dropped in for a little conversation. As far as he knew, she wasn't dating anyone. Maybe she got lonely.

He couldn't just drop in, however. That wouldn't be kosher. He should call first.

He let the phone ring four times. When the answering machine picked up, he broke the connection. He couldn't think of anything to say. He thought it was too bad she wasn't at home, as she was missing a real treat. His new songs were really quite good, even if he did say so himself. And he did have to say so himself, since nobody else would. He supposed others either had poor ears for music or were jealous of his musical abilities.

He went back to the kitchen, stacked the pizza box on a pile with three or four others, and got his guitar out of the chair to do a little more practicing on his new song.

The ringing of the telephone hadn't bothered Jennifer. She told Sherm to go check the caller ID and listen for a message. While he was gone, she stood and glared at Sally.

"Well?" Jennifer said when Sherm returned.

"No message," he said, and Sally was relieved to hear that he could speak. She didn't know why she was relieved, but his silence had been somehow disconcerting.

"Caller ID?" Jennifer asked.

"Somebody named Benton."

Sally was curious as to why Seepy Benton would be calling her, but it didn't seem important under the circumstances. What was important was to get her hands and feet free. She had been straining against the duct tape, testing it, however, and it was wrapped too tightly to give her any chance of escape at all.

Sally thought about Jack's cat and wished Lola were more like him. Hector was so vicious that he would by now have shredded Sherm's pants and maybe severed Jennifer's tendons at the ankle. Lola, on the other hand, was cowering beneath the bed, ready to give a savage hiss if anyone came close to her but not to do anything of practical use.

On the floor beside the chair where Sally more or less sat lay a coil of rope that

Sherm had brought in from somewhere. Sally supposed it had been lying out of sight when Sherm and Jennifer had stood at her door. She felt like a fool for having let them inside, but who would ever have thought that they were planning to hang her?

She would have known if she'd seen the rope, in one end of which a hangman's noose had already been tied.

The only thing that seemed to be delaying the hanging, in fact, was that Sherm and Jennifer couldn't think of a good place to do it.

"I think the front yard would be best," Jennifer said.

"Too much risk," Sherm told her. "Neighbors."

"We want people to see her, so they'll get the message that witches aren't to be tolerated."

"We don't want anybody to see *us*."

"Right." Jennifer nodded. "You're right. We'll have to do it in the back yard."

Sally knew that wouldn't work. While her back fence was lined with oleanders and while there were a couple of crepe myrtles in her back yard, there were no trees. But she wasn't going to mention that. Let Sherm and Jennifer discover it for themselves.

Sherm was the one who found out. Jennifer sent him to check the yard, and when he came back inside, he said, "No trees."

While he could talk, Sally thought, he didn't talk much. She wondered if maybe he wasn't as enthusiastic about the idea of hanging a witch as his wife was. He still had the knife in one hand, and he still looked menacing. But he didn't look like a killer. Not that Sally knew what a killer looked like. The few she'd known had looked about like everyone else. So she supposed Sherm did look like a killer after all.

And so did Jennifer, who had that feverish look back in her eyes. Sally was convinced that the two of them had killed Harold Curtin, probably after Jennifer had found out he was attending witch meetings. Jennifer wouldn't like that at all, and she would like it even less that she'd been working with him, possibly becoming contaminated by the very presence of a man who had worshipped Satan and participated in whatever barbaric rites the Houston coven practiced.

Considering what Vera had told her, Sally was sure the idea of barbaric rites was pretty far-fetched, but she didn't think

Jennifer would see it that way. Any rites at all would seem barbaric to her.

"What kind of back yard doesn't have trees?" Jennifer said.

"Mine," Sally said.

"Put some tape over the witch's mouth," Jennifer told Sherm. "I'm tired of listening to her."

Sherm did as he was told. The upside was that he had to put the knife down on the coffee table to apply the tape, and when he was finished, he didn't bother to pick up the knife again, though it wasn't doing Sally any good where it was.

With her mouth taped, Sally found it difficult to breathe. She wasn't bothered with the allergies that afflicted many people living in Hughes, so maybe it was just the thought that she couldn't open her mouth that was distressing her.

"*Ummmmmmmmpf,*" she said.

"Shut up," Jennifer said. "You're already causing us enough trouble."

"*Ummmmmmmmpf.*"

Jennifer slapped her. Sally was getting really tired of that, but she managed to fall out of the chair and hit the coffee table. Unfortunately, she didn't knock the coffee table over or even unbalance it, so the knife still lay on it.

She wasn't sure she could have done anything with the knife even if she'd gotten hold of it, since her hands were behind her and she had just about lost the feeling in them. The duct tape had cut off the circulation to her fingers.

"Pick her up, Sherm," Jennifer said.

Sherm put his hands under her arms and jerked her off the floor. He tossed her back into the chair.

"What about her closet?" Jennifer said. "People hang themselves in closets all the time, don't they?"

If they did, Sally wasn't aware of it. The curse of being an English teacher was that all she could think of was a play by Arthur Kopit, *Oh, Dad, Poor Dad, Mama's Hung You in the Closet, and I'm Feeling So Sad.* The play was nearly fifty years old by now and mostly forgotten. Sally felt that she was no doubt the only person in the world who was thinking of it at that moment. And probably the only one about to be hanged, too.

Sherm said, "I don't think a closet pole will hold her."

Sally wasn't certain whether that was a comment on her weight or the closet pole. Sure, she was two pounds above the ideal for her age and height, maybe three at the most. Or four. But that was all. So Sherm must have meant that the pole itself was none too sturdy. And he was right about that.

"And it would be too low," Sherm added. He was growing downright garrulous.

"Shower-curtain rod?" Jennifer said.

"Wouldn't hold her."

"Check it anyway."

He wasn't going to have any luck, though Sally wouldn't have told him that even if she could have.

Sherm wandered off. Jennifer stood and watched Sally with her hot eyes. Sally hoped Jennifer didn't decide to snatch up the knife and finish things the easy way.

Sherm came back into the room. "She has tub enclosures with those sliding glass doors."

"Well, think of something!" Jennifer said.

If Sally had been a gambler, she'd have bet that thinking wasn't Sherm's strong suit. No wonder Jennifer was the salesperson in their business. But a salesperson needed patience, and Jennifer's seemed to be wearing thin.

"We have to hang her somewhere," Jennifer said.

Sally wanted to say, "No, you don't," but

all she could manage was *"Ummmmm-mmmpf."*

"Shut up," Jennifer said.

She stood with her hands on her hips, looking around the room. She stopped looking when she saw the ceiling fan. She pointed to it and said, "We'll hang her from that."

Sherm looked doubtful. "Might not hold."

"You know it will. When ours was installed, they cut through the Sheetrock and were careful to screw the base of the fan into something real solid in the attic."

Really solid, Sally wanted to say. *"Ummmmmpf"* was all she managed.

"Doesn't mean hers is the same as ours," Sherm told Jennifer.

"You're either part of the solution, Sherm, or you're part of the problem. Which is it going to be?"

"Ceiling fan is okay with me."

"Good. Now hoist her up there."

Sherm turned a critical gaze on Sally.

"Won't be easy."

If the whole thing hadn't been so ridiculous, Sally would have been insulted.

"Might need a step stool," Sherm said.

"Just get a chair, Sherm. You can lift her. She's not that big."

Gee, thanks, Sally thought.

Sherm went to the kitchen and brought back one of the wooden chairs. After setting it underneath and a little to the right of the ceiling fan, he pulled Sally up and dragged her over to it. Jennifer trailed along behind them.

When Sherm got to the chair, he said, "Hold her," and he shoved Sally at Jennifer, who staggered as she took Sally's weight.

Sherm went and got the rope. He stepped up into the chair and tied the rope around the short rod that connected the fan blades to the base.

"Hurry up, Sherm," Jennifer said. "She's heavy."

Sally made a promise to herself that if she ever got loose, she was going on a diet.

Sherm got the rope tied to the fan. He took hold of it and swung himself out of the chair. When he stopped swinging, he hung from the rope for a few seconds.

"See?" Jennifer said. "I told you it would hold. Now get down from there and hang her."

Sherm dropped to the floor and then got back on the chair. Jennifer pushed Sally toward him, and he slipped his hands under her armpits.

Sally knew that she wasn't likely to have another chance to get away, so she twisted herself as hard as she could. Sherm hadn't been expecting anything, and he dropped her.

When she hit the floor, Sally started off toward the coffee table, where the knife still lay. She was on her side, ooching herself along the rug with her shoulder while she pushed with her feet. She moved faster than she thought she would, but then she was desperate.

Even in desperation, however, she wasn't moving fast, so she didn't get far. Jennifer caught up with her and took hold of her hair.

"This is going to hurt," Jennifer said, sounding all too happy about it, and she dragged Sally back to the chair.

It did hurt, too, a lot, and tears came to Sally's eyes. She couldn't cry out, which was just as well. The noise might have made Jennifer even angrier.

Jennifer stood Sally up, not an easy job, as Sally went limp. If they were going to hang her, they were going to have to work at it.

After a considerable struggle, Jennifer got Sally upright, and Sherm took her. This time he was ready, and when she tried to squirm away, he didn't lose his hold. He moved over in the chair, holding her with one arm while he worked the hangman's noose over her head. He pulled it tight and stepped down to the floor.

Sally had quit squirming. She didn't want to give them any help by hanging herself before they got ready.

"What about a note?" Sherm said.

"No note," Jennifer said. "She wouldn't write one anyway, and we don't want people to think it's a suicide."

"I know that. I was thinking about a note from you about how she had been tried and convicted."

"No. We don't want to leave any more evidence than we have to."

Sally didn't know a great deal about police work, but she knew they'd already left plenty of evidence. Jennifer's fingerprints would be all over the duct tape, and Sherm's would be on the chair. The rope could probably be traced. They might even forget to pick up the knife from the coffee table.

"How will people know why she's been hung?"

Hanged, you moron, Sally thought.

"The whole town knows she's a witch, Sherm."

"But what if they think she did it herself?"

"Nobody's going to think that. Stop all the arguing and move the chair."

Sally thought that Sherm didn't really want to go through with it. Now that they'd come to the crucial moment, he couldn't bring himself to kill her.

Sally couldn't believe it was going to happen, either. Even when they'd taped her hands and feet and mouth, she couldn't believe it. Maybe, she thought, the hardest thing to accept in the whole of existence is that you're about to become something other than a part of that existence.

Sally thought about Sarah Good and the other women who'd been executed in Salem all those years ago. How must they have felt? Surely most if not all of them believed in their own innocence and knew the injustice of what was about to happen to them. They must have wondered how blame had come to fall on them. They must have wondered how they could possibly be about to lose their lives for something of which they were entirely innocent. There was no one to speak up for them then, however, just as there was no one to speak up for Sally now. They had been condemned, and they were going to hang.

And yet they must have believed that

they would somehow escape. That they wouldn't die at the end of a hangman's noose. Certainly Sally believed that she was going to escape, no matter how things might seem to be headed in another direction. She would escape, and then she would make Jennifer and Sherm sorry they had ever messed with her.

"You sure about this?" Sherm asked Jennifer.

"Of course I'm sure. This woman's done harm to you and me and to all the people of this community, and she's gotten away with it. She wants to destroy the minds of the children with satanic books. Plus, she's an evil woman, descended from an evil woman. She deserves what she's getting, and nobody's going to give it to her if we don't. Everybody resigned from the Mothers Against Witchcraft today because of the scene she made last night. No one will stand up for the right except us. And that's exactly what we're going to do. What's right."

"Are you sure it's right?"

"Absolutely. It has to be done, and we're going to do it right now. Move the chair."

Sherm didn't look too happy about it.

"If you say so."

Sherm took hold of the back of the chair.

"Ummmmmmmpf!" Sally said.

"Do it, Sherm," Jennifer said. "If you don't, I will."

"I don't like it," Sherm said, but even as he said it, he jerked the chair from beneath Sally's feet.

28

After thinking it over, Seepy Benton decided that Sally must have gone out to eat and that she would be coming back to her house soon. He thought it would be okay to drop by, and if she was surprised to see him, he could tell her that he had called and gotten no answer. If she wasn't there, he could just come on back home. So he put on a fresh aloha shirt, a green one with parrots that were yellow and red and blue. He thought it looked pretty darned spiffy, as did the wide-brimmed, flat-crowned hat he put on his head.

Looking at himself in the mirror he wondered if he might be just a tad too rabbinical, so he changed to a western straw hat that gave him what he believed to be the look of an authentic singing cowboy.

Roy Rogers, eat your heart out, he thought.

The cats had come out of hiding, and, not seeing the guitar, they had gone to their four food bowls and begun to eat.

When Seepy came into the kitchen, carrying his nylon guitar case, the cats gave him a startled look and scampered away.

"I'm not going to play," Seepy said, a little disappointed in them, though he knew you couldn't really expect a cat to appreciate poetry and a beautiful melody. "I'm going out for a while. You guys will have to fend for yourselves." He always referred to the cats as *guys* even though Emily clearly wasn't. "You can come on out now."

The cats had been fooled before, however, and they remained in hiding.

"All right, if that's the way you feel, stay where you are."

Seepy went out the back door to his car, a sensible Saturn instead of a trusty steed like Trigger or Champion. He put the guitar in the backseat. He thought that Sally would like his songs if she'd just listen to them. She was an English teacher, after all, and English teachers were supposed to like poetry, unlike certain cats he could name. And the musical accompaniment just made the poetry that much better.

He had checked Sally's address in the faculty address book before leaving, and he knew her house wasn't far, not that anything in Hughes was very far from anything else. He hoped that Sally was back from dinner, and he was already looking forward to their visit.

It took him only a few minutes to get to the house. It appeared at first glance to be dark, but he parked at the curb and got out anyway. Since he was already there, he might as well try the door.

After he got the guitar out of the backseat, he noticed that the house wasn't entirely dark, after all. The plantation shutters were closed, but not so tightly that little strips of light didn't shine through. Seepy thought that Sally just liked her privacy. He got a good grip on the handle of his guitar, squared his shoulders, and strode up the walk. Roy Rogers would have been proud.

When he reached the door, he set down the guitar and rang the bell.

Sherm, not being a professional hangman, had made one serious miscalculation, and Sally was grateful for it.

When he'd tied the rope to the fan, he'd left it just a little bit too long. So when he moved the chair from beneath Sally's feet, her toes actually came in contact with the rug.

The shock of the drop had been bad, as had the burn of the rope on her neck, which felt as if it had stretched a foot or so. But her neck wasn't broken, mainly because she hadn't come to a sudden stop at the end of the rope. She had, in a manner of speaking, landed on her feet. Or her toes. She was able to balance there for a second or two at a time like a ballerina with an inner-ear problem, just enough to keep from strangling.

"Look what you've done, Sherm," Jennifer said. "She's not dead."

Sally didn't see or hear Sherm's reaction, if he had one. She was too busy trying to maintain her balance.

"We have to do something," Jennifer said.

"What?" Sherm asked.

"Go over there and hang on to her. That way she'll choke to death."

Sherm said he didn't want to do that.

Jennifer insisted.

Sherm gave in and started toward Sally.

Then the doorbell rang.

Seepy knew that someone was inside Sally's house. He could hear voices. They were muffled, so he couldn't tell if one of them was Sally's. He wondered if she might still be gone. What if burglars had closed the shutters so they couldn't be seen while they took Sally's TV, VCR, DVD player, computer, and all the other things that burglars took?

Seepy knew he wasn't really Roy Rogers, or even Gabby Hayes, but he couldn't allow burglars to make off with Sally's property. He set down his guitar case and pushed the bell button again and again.

"Who *is* that?" Jennifer said.

Sherm shrugged. "Maybe he'll leave."

The bell kept ringing.

"Go to the door, Sherm. And be careful. Don't show your face, and don't let anybody in. We can't afford to let anybody see us."

"I know that," Sherm said.

He went to the door and opened it, leaving the safety chain on as Sally had done earlier.

"Yes?" he said, staying behind the door and out of Seepy's sight. "What can I do for you?"

"I'm here to see Miss Good," Seepy said.

"She's busy right now. She doesn't want to see you."

Seepy couldn't see who was doing the

talking, and he didn't believe that Sally didn't want to see him. She hadn't even known he was coming. He craned his neck, trying to see into the room.

"She asked me to stop by," Seepy said. He picked up the nylon guitar case. "She wanted to hear some of the new songs I've written."

"Well, she must have made a mistake telling you that," Sherm said. "She invited us over."

"Who's *us?*"

"None of your business," Sherm said.

He started to close the door, but Seepy got his shoe in the crack.

"What's all that noise?" Seepy said.

The noise was Sally, who was dancing around on her toes and making the loudest noises she could with the duct tape across her mouth.

"It sounds like someone's in trouble," Seepy said. "I'm coming in."

"No. You can't do that."

Seepy shoved on the door with his shoulder. It stopped at the end of the chain. Seepy thought he saw movement in the room, as if someone else had come to the door. The noises from inside the house got a bit louder.

Seepy took a step back. As Sherm tried

again to close the door, Seepy rammed into it with his shoulder.

Seepy was not a small man, and he worked out for an hour a day on his home gym.

Sherm, on the other hand, was small and didn't work out at all. The door smacked him in the face, and the screws of the safety chain pulled out of the wall.

Seepy went through the door, carrying his guitar case and looking around for Sally.

He didn't see her at first. Instead he saw Sherm, who was holding his hands over his nose. Blood was coming from between his fingers.

"I didn't mean to hurt you," Seepy said, just before he saw Jennifer, who was coming at him with a knife raised above her head. If her hair had been in a bun, she would have been a dead ringer for the deranged Anthony Perkins in *Psycho*.

As she brought the knife down, Seepy put his guitar case up to protect himself. The knife sliced through the nylon and crunched through the wooden base of the guitar with a sound that would have broken Seepy's heart in a different situation. As it was, he didn't have time to think about it. He twisted the guitar case, jerking the knife, which was still embedded in the guitar, out of Jennifer's hand.

As he turned the case over to remove the knife, he saw Sally dangling at the end of the rope.

"Holy crap!" he said.

He wrenched the knife from the case just as Jennifer and Sherm landed on his back.

Sally had no idea what Seepy Benton was doing in her house, but she was happy to see him, even if he had ruined her door frame. But it didn't seem that he was going to be able to do much for her, as now he was rolling around on the floor beneath a pile of Jacksons, who seemed intent on getting their knife back from him and then, no doubt, cutting his throat or something equally messy, unless Sally could do something about it.

She thought she had noticed that the fan above her was beginning to give way. Maybe if she bounced around some more, it would tear loose from the ceiling. Then, if it didn't kill her when it fell, maybe she could do something to help Seepy, who seemed to be getting the worst of it.

Jennifer Jackson was kicking and spitting like a cat, and Sherm was trying to get a grip on Seepy's neck to choke him.

Sally jumped up and down, straining against the rope, abrading the skin of her neck, which was rubbed raw already. A little more skin loss wouldn't look any worse. She'd just have to wear turtlenecks for a while. No scarves, however, though that's what her mother would no doubt have suggested.

The fan was definitely loosening. Sally jumped up and down again, and with a loud squeal the rod holding it to the base on the ceiling tore away. Sally threw herself to the side as the fan crashed to the floor, breaking a couple of the wooden blades.

Sally lay still for a second, and then, somehow, she managed to get to her knees. With a little fancy maneuvering, she got the rope to slip off the rod. After doing that, she hopped on her knees over to Seepy where Jennifer Jackson had gotten hold of the knife and rolled away.

Jennifer got to her feet, and whirled around, looking even more crazed. She brought the knife around in a wide arc, slashing at Sally's face. Sally leaned back. Before Jennifer could recover from the swing, Sally lunged forward and butted her in the abdomen.

Thrown off-balance, Jennifer stumbled over Sherm and Seepy and fell, hitting the back of her head hard against the floor. Her eyes rolled up into her head, and the knife dropped from her limp fingers.

Sherm turned away from Seepy to look at Sally, his face a bloody mask. She didn't feel a bit sorry for him, and she fell across the back of his legs.

He loosened his grip on Seepy's neck to make a grab for Sally, who rolled up to his thighs, throwing him forward across Seepy.

As Seepy squirmed out from under Sherm, Sally moved up onto Sherm's back, pinning him to the floor.

Seepy got to his feet and looked around. When he saw Jennifer, he picked up the knife that lay beside her. Then he cut the tape that bound Sally's feet and ankles. He didn't try to cut the rope. He loosened the noose and pulled it over her head, tossing the rope aside.

"You can get up now," he said.

Sally wasn't sure she could. She just rolled off Sherm and lay on her back on the floor.

Seepy reached down to pull the tape from her mouth.

Sally wanted to tell him to be careful, but all she could say was *"Ummmmmpf."*

Seepy grabbed one end of the tape and jerked as hard as he could. It made a loud ripping sound as it came away from her face.

"*EEEEyooooooow!*" Sally said.

"My feelings exactly," Seepy told her.

29

"Are you sure you don't want to go to the emergency room?" Seepy asked.

Sally said she was sure.

"The EMTs fixed me up just fine."

Her throat was greasy with antibiotic ointment, and she'd been given some anti-inflammatory pills, three of which she'd taken. The EMTs had also checked her for a concussion, but she'd been fine in that respect.

"You sound like that singer from when I was a lot younger. What was her name?"

Sally said she didn't know.

" 'Bette Davis Eyes.' That one. Remember?"

"Kim Carnes," Sally said, her voice rasping out.

Her throat didn't feel quite as bad on the inside as her neck looked on the outside, but it was sore.

"That's her," Seepy said. "Kim Carnes. How could I have forgotten."

They were in Sally's den. Sally was on

the couch, and Seepy was in a chair, holding his straw hat, which had been crushed in his struggle with the Jacksons. His guitar case was on the floor beside him. He hadn't looked inside it.

Lola was lying on top of the guitar case, shedding all over the nylon. She had come out from under the bed only after the police had left. She had looked around as if to check on what all the fuss had been about, and her eye had settled almost at once on the guitar case. She took it over at once, in spite of Seepy's proximity. It had taken her a while to get used to him, as he didn't seem bothered at all by her hissing. After a while she'd given up on trying to intimidate him, curled into a calico ball, and gone to sleep.

"It sounds kind of sexy," Seepy said. "Kim Carnes's voice, I mean. Yours, too."

Sally supposed he was either trying to compliment her or make her feel better, but she didn't care how she sounded. She was tired, her living room was a mess, she was going to have to get a new ceiling fan, the door frame would need repair and paint, and she hurt all over. Her neck was bruised and sore both inside and out, and she had a knot on her forehead, an aching shoulder, and rug burns on her knees.

"I think that policeman is a little upset with you," Seepy said.

Sally knew that he was referring to Lieutenant Weems, who had arrived shortly after the uniformed officers.

"He's always upset with somebody," Sally said.

She had given a long statement to Weems, who somewhere in the course of it had told her that the Jacksons had admitted that they'd met with the Garden Gnome the night of his death. They had not, however, admitted killing him.

Sally had pointed out that they'd certainly tried to kill her, and she'd explained her theory that they'd killed Curtin because of his association with witchcraft.

"They're a little crazy on the subject," Sally had said, touching her throat with her fingertips.

Weems had agreed with her about the craziness of the Jacksons, but he'd gone on to say something about the difference in the MO in the two instances.

"I'm wondering why they didn't hang Curtin. If they thought that was the right thing to do to witches, why not hang him, too?"

"You saw him," Sally had said. "He was short, but he was stocky. He must weigh a lot more than I do." She didn't know that was true, but she hoped it was. "I don't think Sherm could have handled him, even with Jennifer's help. I don't think they could have handled me if they hadn't bonked me in the head with the door."

Seepy had broken in at that point to mention the knife.

Weems was of the opinion that the knife might have worked if they'd threatened Curtin with it, but he'd added that the knife might not have been necessary because "Curtin was so plotzed he probably didn't know whether he was drinking water, poison, or bourbon."

Sally concluded that the Jacksons had poisoned Curtin rather than hanging him because it had been a lot easier than hoisting him to the ceiling fan, and he might not even have had one. She pointed out that it wasn't as easy to hang someone as people might think.

"After all, they tried to do it to me, and it didn't work."

Seepy had eyed the rope burns on her neck.

"You're going to look a little like Clint Eastwood in that movie. What was it?"

"*Hang 'Em High*," Weems said.

Sally recalled having spoken that very

sentence to Christopher Matthys. She wished now she'd never said it.

"That's the one," Seepy said. "I don't know how I could have forgotten the name. Inger Stevens is in it, too. That's a good movie."

After Weems agreed with him, Seepy launched into a discussion of the Billy Jack movies. Sally had no idea how they'd gotten so far off the subject, and when Seepy started to proclaim the glories of *Billy Jack Goes to Washington*, she tried to bring the subject back to the Jacksons.

"I'm sorry to interrupt," she said to Weems, who looked grateful. "But do you think the Jacksons are the ones who killed Harold Curtin? Or not?"

Weems wasn't sure.

"They might be nuts on the subject of witchcraft, but they were working together with Curtin on this bond issue thing. Why kill your friends?"

Sally had an answer. "Because they found out he was a member of a coven of witches. They didn't want to be contaminated by the association."

While admitting that it all fit together neatly, Weems hadn't been entirely convinced. Now, thinking it over in the relative calm after the attempted hanging, Sally

322

wasn't so sure, either. It seemed to her that she'd missed something along the way, some small but essential clue. Or rather, she hadn't missed it but had just over-looked it. She'd felt that way before, but whatever was bothering her still hadn't surfaced, and with the bump on the head she'd gotten from the door, she was think-ing less clearly than usual. She wished Jack were there. She could have talked the whole thing over with him. Seepy Benton was nice enough, but he just wasn't the same.

Good grief, she thought. Could I pos-sibly be jealous of Vera?

No, she told herself, that wasn't it. She was happy for Jack, and for Vera, too. She had just become accustomed to talking things over with Jack, and she could still do that. The fact that he and Vera were a couple now didn't change anything as far as their friendship went.

Or maybe, Sally thought, it wasn't Jack and Vera. Maybe something else was both-ering her. Maybe Jack had some connection to that clue she couldn't quite remember.

"Your cat likes my guitar case," Seepy said, breaking into her thoughts.

Sally looked over at Lola, who appeared to have settled herself down for the night.

"I'm sorry that she's shedding on it," Sally said.

Lola heard. As if she knew they were talking about her, she looked up and said, *"Rrrrrrr."*

"I know *you're* not sorry," Sally said. "That's why I was apologizing for you."

"Meow," Lola said.

"You talk to your cat," Seepy said, not appearing in the least surprised.

"Yes. Sometimes I forget she's just a cat."

"I talk to mine, too." Seepy paused. "I have four."

Maybe Seepy wasn't so bad after all, Sally thought. But that wasn't going to help her remember whatever it was that she needed to remember.

"You're probably wondering why I came by," Seepy said. "It wasn't to talk about cats."

Sally already knew why he'd come to see her. She said, "I heard what you told Lieutenant Weems."

"Oh." Seepy gave his guitar case a wistful glance. "Well, I guess you won't have to listen to me pick and sing. I won't be playing that guitar for a while, not with a knife in its back. I'm almost afraid to look at it." He brightened. "But I have another one at home. Two more, in fact."

Sally thought he must want her to ask him to come by again some other time and to bring one of his other guitars. But she couldn't bring herself to do it.

"Have I thanked you for rescuing me?"

Seepy laughed. "I didn't rescue you." He looked at her door. "All I did was mess up your wall. You're the one who rescued me. Sherm Jackson had me in a death grip."

"You distracted them and gave me time to get loose. Well, sort of loose."

"I wish I could take credit for saving you, but I don't think it would be right. However, if you're feeling grateful to me . . ."

Sally knew she'd made a big mistake, but there was nothing to do now. She'd have to bite the bullet and say what he wanted to hear. Well, almost.

"Why don't you come by my office tomorrow and play one of your new songs for me."

"You're going to be at school tomorrow?"

"I don't miss school if I can walk and talk."

"You can barely talk. Tomorrow you might be even worse."

"Thanks for the encouragement."

Seepy stood up. "I'm sure you'll be fine. When are your office hours?"

"The afternoon might be best," Sally told him, thinking that there would be fewer people in the building at that time.

"Great. I'll be there around three. Will that be all right?"

"Sounds fine. I'm looking forward to it."

Sally, she thought, you are such a liar.

Seepy reached for his guitar case. Lola roused herself and hissed at him.

"Lola," Sally said. "Get off the case."

Lola hissed again.

"Lola."

Lola stood up, humped her back, and stretched out her front legs. She scratched the guitar case, tentatively at first, then more vigorously.

"Lola!"

The scratching slowed down. Lola turned her head slowly and looked up at Sally.

"Meow?"

"Get down. Now."

"Meow."

Lola got off the guitar case, but she took her time about doing it, grooming herself a little before finally moving to the floor.

Seepy reached for the case.

"Meowrrrrrr."

"I'm taking the case," Seepy told her. "You got to have a nice nap on it, and now it's time for me to go home. You'll be glad when I've gone."

"Meow."

"That's what I thought," Seepy said.

Seepy picked up his guitar case. Now he had a ruined guitar case in one hand and a battered straw hat in the other, like some itinerant minstrel from the 1930s. Except for the shirt. Sally was sure that no one in the 1930s had ever worn a shirt quite as bright as the one Seepy wore. She wondered where he found such wild shirts.

"Good night, Sally," Seepy said. "Good night, Lola."

"Good night," Sally said. "Thanks for coming by in time."

"Glad to be of help."

"Meow," Lola said, and Seepy left them there.

Sally went into the bedroom, ready for a hot shower and some sleep. She looked at herself in the full-length mirror on the inside of the closet door.

She didn't look as bad as she'd thought. No, the awful truth was that she looked even worse. Maybe in addition to the turtleneck, she should wear a paper bag over her head.

When she started to get undressed, the

telephone rang. Sally looked at the caller ID.

The call was from her mother.

Lola peered out from under the bed. Sally looked at her and said, "The perfect end to a perfect day."

"Meow," said Lola.

From Cotton Mather's
The Wonders of the Invisible World

If a drop of innocent blood should be shed, in the prosecution of the witchcrafts among us, how unhappy are we!

30

When Sally got to her office the next morning, Troy Beauchamp was standing at the door.

"Tell me everything," he said.

Sally had no idea how he'd already heard about her adventures. It was as if he picked up gossip out of the air. Or maybe he talked to her mother.

Sally unlocked the door and went inside. Troy was right behind her, so as soon as she put down her books, she told him an abbreviated version of the story.

"Details," he said. "I want details."

Sally gave him a few, and he left. She wondered if he would teach class at all that day or if he'd simply spend his time going from one office to another, spreading the news.

While he was doing that, Sally checked to see if she had any messages. She didn't, so she picked up the phone and called Wynona.

"Wussup?" Wynona said when she answered the ring.

Sally thought Wynona really could use a refresher course in telephone etiquette.

"Have you heard from Ellen Baldree today?" Sally asked.

"She called to let me know she'd be here. I haven't actually seen her."

Sally thanked her and hung up. She wasn't surprised that Ellen hadn't called her. At least she'd gotten in touch with someone, and Sally wouldn't have to worry about meeting the classes for her.

Almost as soon as Sally put the phone back on the hook, Jack showed up. He looked tired, and Sally was sure that he and Vera had made up their differences.

Jack didn't have Troy's sources, and he seemed a little taken aback at her appearance.

"Were you in a car wreck?" he said.

Sally's forehead was bruised, and her face was a little puffy. When she talked, she sounded as if she had a terrible cold.

"It wasn't a car wreck," she said. "Someone tried to hang me."

"You're joking, right?"

"I wouldn't joke about a thing like that. Jennifer and Sherm Jackson tried to hang me. Literally."

"Why?"

"For the crime of witchcraft."

Jack sat in the chair by her desk and asked her to tell him all about it.

"If it doesn't hurt too much to talk," he added.

"It's not so bad. My mother recommended hot tea with lemon and honey. It actually helped."

"Did she recommend the scarf?"

Sally touched the scarf. "Yes. I was planning to wear a turtleneck sweater, but it's too hot for that, and none of my summer things have turtlenecks."

"The scarf makes you look, oh, I don't know. Kind of exotic."

"Yes, like Isadora Duncan. Remember that story? There was a movie about her."

"With Vanessa Redgrave. I saw it when I was a kid. But you shouldn't be so paranoid. Cars don't have spoked wheels these days."

"I'm not paranoid. The scarf makes me feel old."

"Then I guess you wouldn't be wearing it if your neck weren't in bad shape. So tell me about it."

Sally gave him an abbreviated version of the events, with fewer details than Troy had demanded.

"Wow," he said when she had finished. "You really weren't kidding. You're lucky to be alive."

"I don't know that I'd have made it if Seepy hadn't arrived when he did."

Jack smiled. "You and Seepy, huh?"

"No, not me and Seepy. He's very nice, and he may even have saved my life, but I'm not sure I need to hear him sing his songs. I don't care if he sounds like Johnny Cash."

"He does have a deep voice," Jack said. "But there was only one Johnny Cash, and now he's gone. Seepy can't even come close."

"You've heard him?"

"I don't have to hear him to know that."

"You could come by this afternoon at three. He'll be here for a serenade."

"Lucky you. You get your life saved, and then you get songs composed in your honor. But the best thing is that you've put two more killers behind bars."

"They put themselves there. And to tell the truth, I'm not sure they're killers."

Sally had thought everything over before she went to sleep the previous evening. She'd thought she'd fall asleep as soon as she lay down, but it hadn't worked out that way. Even the pain pills she'd taken hadn't had much of an effect. She'd lain awake for quite a while, and the events of the past few days had paraded themselves through her head. A couple of things had been explained. She had found out who had sent the e-mail about her, and she knew why Harold Curtin had spent some time with a witches' coven. She even thought that she knew why Curtin had been killed. But Weems wasn't convinced, and when Sally thought about his arguments, she could see why.

Jennifer and Sherm had been intent on going by the book when it came to hanging her, or at least Jennifer had. It did seem logical that if they'd executed the Garden Gnome for witchcraft, they'd have done it the right way.

And there was something Jennifer had said, something that Sally had forgotten to tell Weems. Sally couldn't remember the exact words, having been occupied with trying to survive at the time they'd been spoken, but they had something to do with the fact that Jennifer didn't want people to think Sally's death was a suicide.

If Jennifer didn't want Sally's death to look like a suicide, then why had she and Sherm killed Curtin in a way that made people think of suicide immediately?

Sally didn't have an answer, and she had called Weems before leaving for school to ask him if he had one.

He didn't, but he'd reminded Sally again

that he didn't think the Jacksons were guilty of Curtin's death.

"So there's still a killer out there somewhere," Sally had said. "And we're right back where we started."

"There's no *we*," Weems had told her. "I don't want you getting mixed up in this again. You've done enough damage already, and you've nearly gotten yourself killed in the process. Just relax and let me handle things."

Sally had promised that she would, and she tried not to think about the case anymore. But she found that she couldn't help herself.

"Are you still there?" Jack said, waving his hand in front of her face.

Sally came out of her trance.

"I'm still here. I was just thinking."

"I was worried about you. That knot on your head could be dangerous. Did you have it checked out?"

Sally told him that she was fine and that there was no danger of concussion.

"How many fingers am I holding up?" Jack asked.

"None. Don't be an idiot."

"I'm only trying to help. I'm sorry I wasn't there last night. Even if you aren't sure the Jacksons are killers."

Sally didn't think he would have been much help. She said, "As I recall, the last time you were in danger, I had to do the rescuing."

"Well," Jack said, "Hector helped."

"Lola didn't."

Jack laughed. "Hector is unique. You can't expect any other cat to be as vicious as he is. But tell me one thing."

"About Lola?"

"No. About the Jacksons. You said you weren't sure they were killers. They certainly tried to kill you."

"They were pretty inept when you think about it. But what I meant was that I don't think they killed the Gnome."

"If they didn't, who did?"

"I don't know. And Lieutenant Weems doesn't want me to try to find out. He made that very clear."

"I don't think you're in any condition to be tracking down a killer," Jack said.

"I'm not. It's just that I feel as if I know something that would help, and I can't remember what it is."

"You're too young to be having senior moments," Jack said, standing up. "I have to go get ready for my next class. Can you stay out of trouble for a while?"

"I can manage. What about you? Are

you and Vera getting along now?"

Jack blushed, and Sally knew she'd been right about why he looked tired.

"We're getting along fine," he said.

"Good. I hope you don't spend so much time with her that you forget about your friends."

"Rave on," Jack said. "You don't have to worry about that."

"What did you just say?"

"That you don't have to worry. I'll be hanging around as usual. I'm still your friend."

"Not that. The first part."

"The first part of what?"

"Of what you said. It was a song title."

"Oh, that. I said, 'Rave on.' It's the name of a Buddy Holly song. It begins, 'Rave on, it's a crazy feeling . . .' "

"I know," Sally said, and then everything clicked into place.

31

Harriet Denson had been teaching chemistry at Hughes Community College for as long as anyone there could remember. She was, by at least one year, the ranking member of the faculty, having begun teaching at Hughes in the days when it was Hughes Junior College. She had, in fact, stepped into the Hughes chemistry lab right after her college graduation, thirty-six years earlier.

These days Harriet seemed to carry the smell of the lab with her wherever she went, and Sally could easily understand why, as the entire science building at HCC was pervaded by the odor that seemed peculiar to science buildings everywhere. Sally couldn't identify the smell, but she thought there was a touch of formaldehyde in it, along with whatever else was there.

The smell was strong in Harriet's office, which was almost as cluttered as Sally's. Sally wrinkled her nose.

"You'll get used to it," Harriet said. "God knows, I have. I hardly notice it anymore."

Sally hadn't mentioned the smell, but she supposed others had.

"I like your scarf," Harriet said, courteously failing to mention the bump on Sally's forehead. "Very stylish."

"Thanks," Sally said.

She'd never seen Harriet without some kind of drab lab smock over her clothes. She even wore the smock to faculty meetings and to any function that occurred during the day, from art gallery openings to retirement parties.

"Now, what was it you wanted to ask me about?" Harriet said.

"Cationic detergents," Sally told her, repeating what she'd said on the telephone.

"Oh, yes. Well, as you know, a cation is an ion with a positive charge."

Sally said she hadn't known that. She hadn't made As in her chemistry classes, but she neglected to mention that.

"You don't need to know about cations, I suppose," Harriet said. "After all, I don't know who wrote *Beowulf*."

Sally thought of telling her that nobody knew that, but she refrained. It would only draw things out.

"At any rate," Harriet said, "the cations neutralize the anions in synthetic detergents."

Sally looked blank.

"They remove the static electricity."

"Oh," Sally said. "So that's why fabric softeners are usually cationic detergents. I wonder if Lieutenant Weems knows that."

"I'm afraid I don't know Lieutenant Weems."

"Count yourself lucky. Let's forget about him. I was wondering if cationic detergents were used in other things besides fabric softeners."

"Why, of course. Many of them are derivatives of ammonia, so they have germicidal properties. That makes them perfect for use in hospitals."

That wasn't what Sally had wanted to hear.

"And that's all?"

"Of course not. They have any number of uses. Another one would be in dishwashers."

"Commercial dishwashers?"

"Yes. For the germicidal properties, of course. The commercial varieties might be stronger than anything you'd put in your home dishwasher."

"Of course," Sally said, nodding. "That's

exactly what I wanted to know. Thanks, Harriet."

"You're welcome," Harriet said.

As Sally left the building, she wondered how long it had been since someone had said "you're welcome" to her. It seemed to Sally that the words had almost become extinct, having been replaced by *no problem* or *sure thing* or something equally inane.

She looked at her watch. It was nearly three o'clock. Time for Seepy Benton to drop by the office and serenade her. But she wasn't going to have time to listen. She hoped Jack was still on the campus.

She went by Jack's office before going to her own. He wasn't there. She supposed that he and Vera had more "making up" to do. She went on to her own office, where she found Seepy Benton standing outside the locked door with a guitar case in hand. This one was made of hard plastic that, Seepy said, he wished he'd been carrying when he dropped by her house, as it might have provided more protection against knife attacks.

"I wasn't expecting a knife attack, though," he added.

"Neither was I," Sally said, as she un-locked her office door.

Seepy followed her inside. He looked

around for a place to set his guitar case. Other than the floor, there wasn't one. All available surfaces were covered with books and papers.

"I like your office," Seepy said.

Today he was wearing another aloha shirt, this one covered with brownish-orange pineapples on a purple background.

"Where do you get those shirts?" Sally said.

Seepy put the guitar case on the floor, stood back up, and spread his arms.

"Nifty, huh?"

"Very."

Sally really didn't care about the shirt. She couldn't decide whether to call Lieutenant Weems or not. She was sure that by now he'd gotten a complete lab report on the detergent that had been used, right down to the brand name. Maybe he'd even traced it to its source, in which case she didn't need to be worrying about it. But she couldn't help herself.

Seepy knelt down and unlatched the guitar case. The instrument inside had some sort of sunburst on the front of it. He took it out of the case and told Sally that it was an old Gibson.

"Pretty valuable, too," he added.

He lifted the guitar from the case as he stood up. Then he clipped a small black object on the end of the guitar neck.

"What's that?" Sally said.

"Electronic tuner." Seepy plucked a string and looked at the tuner. "I'm not so good at tuning by ear." He twisted a knob on the neck and plucked the string again. "Sounds fine. Now for the next one."

"As much as I'd like to hear you sing," Sally said, "something's come up. I have to leave the office now."

Seepy looked as if he'd been hit in the head by a sledgehammer.

"What? You can't leave. I was just getting tuned up."

"It's important. I have to go to the Tea Room."

"Tea is that important?"

"It's not about the tea. It has to do with Harold Curtin's murder."

"He was murdered at a tearoom?"

Sally tried not to let her exasperation creep into her voice.

"I'm not talking about *a* tearoom," she told him. "I'm talking about *the* Tea Room."

"Oh," Seepy said. "I had a meeting there with some of the area institutional research directors. If there's anything we directors like, it's good food. But I thought the portions were a little skimpy."

"That's what you get at a tearoom," Sally said. "Skimpy portions. I really do have to go now."

Seepy put his guitar in the case, clicked the latches into place, and stood up.

"Want some company?"

Sally didn't really want or need any company, but she supposed it wouldn't hurt anything for Seepy to tag along.

"You can leave your guitar here," she said. "I always lock my office door."

"I don't have to worry about that," Seepy said. "Molly always locks the door when she leaves, unless I'm there. Sometimes she even locks it then."

"We can go in my car," Sally said, practically shoving Seepy out the door. "The Tea Room closes at two-thirty, and it opens in the evening only if there's a poetry reading."

"Then it's too late," Seepy said. "It's already nearly three-thirty."

"I'm hoping that the owner and a few of the workers stay there to clean the place up. Come on."

Sally led the slow-moving Seepy out of the building to where her Acura was parked.

"I like your car," Seepy said as he climbed into the passenger seat.

"Thanks," Sally said.

She wondered if she might have made a mistake in letting Seepy tag along, but he'd wanted to come, and she couldn't think of any way to get rid of him.

"So this is about the murder?" Seepy said as Sally drove out of the parking lot.

"Yes. It's just something I want to check before I call the police."

"Shouldn't you let the police do the checking?"

Sally knew that the correct answer to that question was *yes*, but she didn't want to call Weems because she didn't want to seem foolish. She could check first and call Weems if she was right. If she was wrong, then she didn't have to call him at all.

"What if no one's there?" Seepy said.

"If that's the case, I'll just have to check out my theory later," Sally told him.

Seepy leaned back against the leather seat.

"That's fine with me," he said.

The Tea Room was closed, but there were several cars parked in back of the restaurant. Sally thought they must belong to the owner and some of the employees, so she parked under the shade of the oak trees and got out.

"How are you going to get in?" Seepy asked, following her to the front entrance.

"I'm going to bang on the door until someone comes," Sally said.

She didn't have to bang on the door, however. Although the CLOSED sign was in the window, the door wasn't locked. Sally opened it and went inside. Rick Centner was standing at the counter behind the cash register.

"Hello, Dr. Good," he said when he saw Sally. "And hello to you, too, Dr. Benton. I'm Rick Centner. I had you for algebra at HCC."

"That was before I became the director," Seepy said. "I don't teach classes these days."

"Congratulations on the promotion," Centner said. "But I hope you didn't come here to celebrate. We've closed for the day."

"We didn't come here to celebrate," Sally said before Seepy could speak. "*I* came to talk to one of your employees."

"Which one?"

"Jerry Ketchum," Sally said.

32

Sally had thought she recognized a former student when she'd gone to the Tea Room with Jack and Vera, but the young man had turned away and hurried off to the kitchen before she had been able to put a name with his face. She was sure now, however, that the former student was Jerry Ketchum.

From the very first, she and Jack had speculated that one of the Garden Gnome's former students might have killed him, though they hadn't been entirely serious.

Yesterday, Larry Lawrence had told her that the anti-bond forces had recruited some students. Jerry might have been one of them. Maybe even the only one. If he'd read about the Citizens for Fiscal Responsibility in the paper and seen Curtin's name, he could have joined in the hopes that he could get close to Curtin and get revenge on him. Just why he'd want revenge wasn't clear to Sally, as Curtin had already left the college, but it seemed like a good theory.

She didn't explain any of that to Rick Centner when he asked her why she wanted to see Jerry.

"I thought I saw him here the other day," she said, "but I wasn't sure. I wanted to talk to him about something that happened at HCC."

Seepy opened his mouth to say something, so Sally used her elbow to give him a discreet nudge in the ribs. She didn't want him blurting out anything about Curtin's murder.

Seepy's teeth clicked together, making Sally think her nudge might not have been as discreet as she'd intended, but Rick didn't seem to notice.

"Jerry works here, all right," Rick said. "I was glad to help him out."

"Help him out?" Sally said.

"He needs a good job as a condition of his parole."

"He's on parole?"

Rick laughed. "Not all former HCC students own Tea Rooms. I think Jerry dropped out of school for some reason. He didn't tell me why. After that, he started doing some drugs. His family wasn't much help, and he moved to Dallas. Got arrested for dealing up there. I think he's been clean since."

Sally thought that depended on how Rick defined *clean*. She could see why Jerry would have had a big grudge against Curtin, even bigger than she'd thought, if he blamed Curtin for his later problems, and especially if even his family had given up on him. They had been supportive for a while, as Sally knew from their threats to sue the college.

"I'd like to talk to him," Sally said. "Is he here?"

"Yes. He's working in the kitchen. I'll take you back."

Rick walked through the vacant Tea Room. Sally started to follow him, but Seepy grabbed her arm.

"What's going on?" he said.

"It's possible that Jerry Ketchum killed Harold Curtin," she said. "I'm going to ask him."

Sally pulled her arm away and followed Rick. Seepy trailed along behind, looking bewildered.

They went through a pair of swinging doors into the kitchen, which could have won an award for cleanliness. Sally had heard that restaurant kitchens were sometimes not as clean as the diners would like, but this place was spotless.

One man was taking a large plastic bag

of trash out the back door, and another was cleaning the big stove top. A woman was working on the deep stainless-steel double sink.

"We're just about done here, Mr. Centner," said the man cleaning the stove.

The man with the trash bag turned and looked to see who was in the kitchen. When he saw Sally, he threw the bag to the floor, blocking the doorway, and ran.

"That's Jerry," Rick said. "What's the matter with him?"

"He doesn't want to talk to me," Sally said.

"I'll go get him," Seepy said, sweeping past Sally.

He ran across the kitchen, dodged the man at the stove, jumped the trash bag, and went after the fleeing Ketchum.

"He's pretty agile for a man his size," Rick said. "I didn't think he'd be able to jump that bag."

Sally hadn't thought so, either, and she didn't like the idea of Seepy chasing after Jerry.

"We'd better go see if he needs help," she said, taking the same path Seepy had taken, except that she moved the bag out of the way instead of trying to jump it.

When she got outside, she saw that

Seepy and Jerry were running down the street. It was a wide, long street that curved a bit, and Sally had a good view of the two running men. To her surprise, Seepy was gaining on Jerry.

She started after them at a brisk walk. She could run, but she didn't think it would be good for her head and bruised throat. Her voice was much better, so much so that the huskiness was hardly noticeable. But that might change if she didn't take care.

Three blocks away, Jerry abruptly veered off the street and into an open lot where a new house was under construction. Seepy went right after him.

Jerry might have escaped if he'd made it into the trees behind the construction site, but he stepped on something that Sally couldn't see, and his leg turned under him. When he fell, Seepy was there to keep him from getting up, using the simple expedient of sitting on him.

The men who had been working on the house gathered around to see what was going on, but Sally wasn't close enough to hear what they were saying. And she couldn't have heard them even if she'd been closer, as she was already calling Lieutenant Weems on her cell phone.

"I didn't know you played guitar," Weems said the next afternoon in Sally's office.

Sally looked at the guitar case that still lay on the floor.

"I don't. Dr. Benton left that here. He's coming by to pick it up later."

He'd also promised to play Sally one of his songs, now that he knew she'd have time to listen. Sally thought that Weems's presence might inhibit Seepy, so for once she was glad to see the lieutenant.

"I guess I owe him one," Weems said. "That guy might have gotten away yesterday if it hadn't been for him."

Sally could tell from Weems's tone that he was giving her a mild rebuke.

"I know I shouldn't have gone to check on my own," she said. "But I didn't really have any kind of proof. There were a lot of things that seemed to connect, but I wasn't sure they did."

"They did," Weems said. "Ketchum's pretty much confessed everything. He saw an ad in the paper for Citizens for Fiscal Responsibility, and he saw Curtin's name in it. He called Curtin and volunteered."

"I'm surprised Curtin let him within a mile."

"So was Ketchum. But he said Curtin

didn't even seem to remember him. That really got to him. Here he'd done all this suffering that he blamed on Curtin, and Curtin didn't even know who he was."

" 'The most unkindest cut of all,' " Sally said.

"Yeah, whatever. Anyway, Ketchum had heard something while he was locked up about how a certain dishwasher detergent was an untraceable poison. You can learn a lot in a prison. As much as you can in a college. Maybe more, but it's not the same kind of thing, and for Ketchum the detergent idea was something he could use. He thought the only problem he might have would be getting Curtin to drink the stuff."

"So the job at the Tea Room was part of a plan."

"Probably not. I don't think Ketchum got the job with the intention of having access to the detergent. But when he got the job, he had what he needed if he ever got the chance to use it. The Citizens for Fiscal Responsibility gave him that chance."

"And getting Curtin to drink poison proved all too easy."

"He was too drunk to know what he was drinking," Weems said. "Ketchum just took advantage of the situation."

"Have you asked the Jacksons if they saw

Jerry at Curtin's place the night he was killed?"

"What, you think I can't do my job?"

"Just asking."

"Of course we checked on that. They left soon after they got there because Curtin was getting drunk. They don't know if Ketchum showed up later or not."

"But we know."

"Yeah. And Ketchum's going back to jail for a long time."

Sally was sorry about that. She was sorry that something that had happened in a classroom with one of her instructors had led to ruining a young man's life and to his killing the teacher he blamed for his academic failure. It was terrible that something like a classroom confrontation could ultimately result in someone's death and the effective end of another's life.

"It's not your fault," Weems said.

"Are you reading my mind?"

"No, but I know how people think. Believe me, if that kid could do what he did to Curtin, he'd have come to a bad end somehow or other. Remember, he'd been in jail before, for drug dealing."

"Maybe if he'd stayed in school, he wouldn't have gone to jail in the first place."

"Maybe. But maybe he'd have found some other reason to drop out and get busted. Don't beat yourself up about it. It's not your fault. You didn't kill anybody. Ketchum did. It was a choice he made."

Sally knew Weems was right, but it didn't make her feel much better about things.

She was about to tell Weems that when Jack stopped by to tell her that things were looking up for the bond issue.

"Troy told me," he said. "He would have told you, but he said you were busy."

"I didn't even see him," Sally said.

"He's pretty sneaky, all right," Jack said with a glance at Weems. "Troy probably doesn't like policemen. Anyway, with the Citizens for Fiscal Responsibility pretty much discredited, the tide's turning our way. Very strongly our way. Fieldstone should be a happy man."

Sally wished she could feel happy, but even Jack's news didn't cheer her up. She wondered if the passage of a bond issue, even though it would affect thousands of students for the better, was worth the human cost.

"The bond would have passed anyway," Jack said.

"First the lieutenant, and now you," Sally said.

"What?"

"Reading my mind."

Jack and Weems looked at each other.

"The clairvoyant twins," Jack said. "We could get up an act."

"Forget it, Neville," Weems said.

"I will. And I think I'll be leaving now."

He went away, and Sally tried to count her blessings. At least she had escaped the fate that had cut short the lives of Sarah Good and the other accused witches in Salem. Sally felt a sympathy with them that would probably show through whenever she taught about the trials in the future.

She was about to ask Weems what he thought would happen to the Jacksons when Seepy Benton appeared. His shirt was covered with silver palm leaves on a black background.

Very restrained, Sally thought.

"I guess I'd better be going," Weems said, standing.

"No, no, stick around," Seepy said. "I'm going to play a song for Dr. Good. You might enjoy it, too."

"What's it called?"

" 'Friends Don't Let Friends Vote Republican.' "

"I wouldn't enjoy it."

Weems stepped past Seepy and out the door, but he paused in the hall.

"You did good yesterday, catching that guy," he said.

Seepy smiled. "I work out on my home gym. I have an elliptical trainer, too. He didn't have a chance."

"Right," Weems said. "Thanks again, Dr. Good."

Then he was gone, and Seepy was unlatching the guitar case. He took out the guitar, and while he was tuning it, he said, "Some people don't like political songs. Maybe you'd rather hear one of my others."

"Such as?"

" 'Fabric Free' is one of my favorites."

"What's that about?"

"It's sort of related to 'clothing optional.' "

"I think we'd better stick with politics," Sally said.

Seepy strummed a chord.

"Fine with me," he said. "Here we go."

"I can hardly wait," Sally told him, and Seepy started to sing.

About the Author

Bill Crider is chair of the English department at Alvin Community College in Alvin, Texas. He is the author of the Sheriff Dan Rhodes series; two mystery series set at small-town colleges — the Professor Sally Good novels and the Carl Burns books; several other mystery series; and three standalone mystery novels. He lives in Alvin with his wife, Judy.

The employees of Thorndike Press hope you have enjoyed this Large Print book. All our Thorndike and Wheeler Large Print titles are designed for easy reading, and all our books are made to last. Other Thorndike Press Large Print books are available at your library, through selected bookstores, or directly from us.

For information about titles, please call:

(800) 223-1244

or visit our Web site at:

www.gale.com/thorndike
www.gale.com/wheeler

To share your comments, please write:

Publisher
Thorndike Press
295 Kennedy Memorial Drive
Waterville, ME   04901